Charlotte
Brides of Fremont County, Book 5
by Cat Cahill

D1736920

Copyright

---

1. http://www.catcahill.com/

Chapter One

CAÑON CITY, COLORADO - Summer 1881

This was not a job he looked forward to, but the money was too good to say no.

Mark Becker leaned against the side of the depot building as the train screeched to a halt. Between the steam billowing from the engine and the cloud of cigar smoke coming from the portly fellow standing in front of him, Mark could barely make out the train itself. Somewhere onboard was the woman he was being paid to discreetly follow about town.

Eager to get on with it, he pushed himself away from the depot and moved toward the train. Passengers had just begun emerging, some greeting those waiting for them on the platform and others moving away from the depot and off into town. They were of all sorts—finely-dressed folks, rougher-looking men, a handful of families.

He knew Miss Charlotte Montgomery the second she stepped from the first car, valise in hand. Her father hadn't time to send a photograph, but she fit the description and was the only moneyed single woman to emerge from the train. The fact of her identity was confirmed when a gentleman in a long coat stepped around her and made his way into the crowd, his eyes searching for someone in particular.

Best to get this over with. The sooner Miss Montgomery found herself weary of life in Cañon City and back on a train East, the sooner Mark could be paid the handsome sum he was promised.

The man in the long coat reached him just as Mark stepped away from the depot building.

"Becker?" he asked, and Mark had to admire the way the man found him almost immediately in such a large group of people.

When Mark nodded, he continued without introducing himself. "I had charge of Miss Montgomery on her journey from Baltimore. Chester Montgomery offers a deposit for your services with more to arrive as the task is complete, or as a month passes, as the case may be." The man extracted an envelope from a pocket and held it out.

He hadn't expected any part of the payment up front. Mark took it, eager to look inside but not about to indulge in that whim out here on the train platform.

The other fellow's handlebar mustache twitched, as if he knew exactly what was going through Mark's mind. "I'm leaving on the first train north tomorrow. In the meantime, I'll be at the nearest boarding house if you find yourself with questions." He tugged at the brim of his hat and then was off, leaving Mark with his envelope and the charge of a twenty-one-year-old, headstrong heiress.

He shoved the envelope into his own pocket, hoping it was enough to procure lodging at whatever fancy establishment Miss Montgomery chose. He searched the crowd for her.

She was nowhere to be seen.

Panic rose in Mark's chest. Montgomery had sought him out particularly for this job, and if he failed—

"Sir. Pardon me. Sir?" A feminine voice, sweet and rich like warm honey, interrupted his search.

Mark turned, and there, standing before him, was the woman for whom he searched. Up close, the dark hair pinned under her hat looked as soft as silk, a pair of brown eyes studied him intently, and perfectly-shaped pink lips parted as she waited for a response.

"Yes?" He had to find the word somewhere in his mind and drag it out. Given her lifetime of living in the utmost comfort and luxury, Mark had expected a pale, pinched girl, terrified of all that stood around her. But Miss Montgomery was none of that.

She was, quite possibly, the most beautiful woman he'd ever laid eyes upon.

And, according to her father, she wasn't to know that Mark had been hired to ensure her safety.

"Oh, good. For a moment, I thought you might be hard of hearing. Or dull-witted." She smiled at him, and he simultaneously wanted to scoop her into his arms and fight off every man within her immediate vicinity—despite the fact that she'd essentially insulted him.

When he said nothing in response, she added, "You *aren't* dull-witted, are you?" She knitted her eyebrows together as she looked him over.

Mark pressed his shoulders back. "I assure you, miss, I am not. Did you need my assistance? I have an urgent—"

Seemingly satisfied with his answer, she gave him that disarming smile again, the one he thought she must have used back in Baltimore to have ten love-sodden men at her beck and call and that now cut him off in the middle of a sentence. "I am in need of lodging. Could you please direct me to a reputable boarding house for ladies?"

"A boarding house?" he repeated, like the dull-witted man she'd assumed he was.

"Yes." A note impatience laced her voice.

Mark bit back his questions. Asking her why she'd want a simple lodging house instead of the nicest hotel in town could give away his identity. "There is a fine one for ladies only on Macon Avenue." He gestured in the general direction. The place was easy enough to find, and was, thankfully, located directly across the road from a gentlemen's boarding house, where he'd already secured a room upon his return to town.

"Thank you, sir." And with a quick nod at him, she was gone.

Mark waited a respectable few seconds before following after her. She had only that one valise with her. Had she already arranged for trunks to be sent up to the boarding house later? No, that was impossible, considering she didn't know where she'd be staying until she had talked to Mark.

As he darted between people to keep up with her, Mark decided Miss Charlotte Montgomery was quite the conundrum. She had all the money in the world, and yet eschewed the finest lodging establishment in town. She must have had wardrobes full of clothing back in Baltimore, but she carried only one bag. And she didn't appear even remotely concerned about the rougher element in town. In fact, as he caught up to her, he thought he saw her nod a greeting to a pair of trail-weary cowboys.

She found the boarding house he'd suggested easily enough, and he paused across the road when she entered. He could hardly follow her inside an establishment only for ladies. Settling himself in for a wait of indeterminate time, Mark wondered if now might be the best opportunity he had to send a telegram to Montgomery's man, informing him of his employer's daughter's precise whereabouts. But not more than a minute after he'd had the thought, Miss Montgomery emerged from the boarding house.

The woman could hardly have had enough time to procure a room and place her valise inside, much less refresh herself or take a rest. Mark bit back a smile as he watched her hurry across the road toward him. He stepped back into the entry of an empty shorefront, but he needn't have feared. She strode by him, eyes forward, as if on a mission.

Leaving his post, Mark hurried after her. Where in the world could she be going? Wherever it was, she must be certain of her destination, as she didn't hesitate even a half-second to reassure herself of her location.

As far as Mr. Montgomery knew—or so he'd relayed to Mark—his daughter had no real reason to be in Cañon City. She'd simply escaped the family home at her first opportunity, purchased a ticket, and boarded a train the following day. Mark didn't ask why Mr. Montgomery already had a man employed in Baltimore to watch his daughter on the train or why she felt the need to travel thousands of miles from home to a lonesome frontier town.

Some things were best left unknown.

His job was only to inform her father of her whereabouts and to ensure she didn't fall into anything questionable or dangerous. It didn't sound too difficult, and the pay was more than Mark had made in any line of work thus far in his life.

But when Miss Montgomery took a sharp left, straight through the doors of Collier's Saloon, Mark wondered if he'd underestimated the ability of a coddled young woman to find trouble.

Chapter Two

SALOONS, CHARLOTTE decided, were both repulsive and exciting.

She stood near the doorway, blinking in the sudden shadowy dark of the place. Smoke curled around her as what seemed like a hundred different pipes and cigars filled the air. It wasn't unlike the dining room in her father's home in Baltimore, after the ladies excused themselves to the drawing room after dinner. Although she doubted Chester Montgomery had ever hosted such a motley assortment of gentlemen in his home. A couple of them eyed her now with undisguised curiosity, but most were far too engaged in their drink or their card games to pay her any mind.

Emboldened, Charlotte lifted her skirts from the sticky floor and made her way to the barkeep, who stood behind a scarred wooden bar. She waited patiently for him to drop a glass of amber liquid in front of a man who looked as if he could barely keep his eyes open. When the barkeeper's gaze found her, Charlotte offered him her most generous smile.

"Good afternoon, sir," she said. "I was hoping—"

"What are you drinking?" he asked abruptly. He didn't return her smile.

"Oh, no thank you. I'm only seeking—"

He slammed an empty glass down on the bar in front of her. Charlotte jumped.

"I wanted to ask—" she started again, but then the man sloshed a few splashes of what she presumed was whiskey into the glass.

He pressed a cork into the bottle, his eyes on her. Perhaps now he would answer her question. "I'm wondering if you might have seen—"

He thrust a hand out, palm up.

Payment. Of course. She ought to have offered that up front. Perhaps she could have saved the man from wasting his whiskey, as she certainly wasn't about to drink it.

Charlotte fished a couple of coins from her reticule, hoping it was enough. The barkeep looked at the money she placed in his hand and raised his eyebrows at it before pocketing both coins.

"I appreciate your time, sir. I'm hoping you might tell if you've seen . . ." She trailed off as the man turned his back and made his way to the far end of the bar, where a fellow who looked as if he hadn't bathed in months had raised his empty glass.

Charlotte sighed and dropped her hands to the edge of the bar, only to quickly remove them once her gloves touched the sticky surface. Now what? The barkeeper was clearly going to be of no help, and the railroad conductor she'd spoken with on her journey here seemed to think that was the sort of person who would know just about everyone in town. Perhaps she could locate another saloon—

"Collier's not the friendliest sort," a male voice said from next to her.

Charlotte nearly jumped at the sound of his voice. She'd been so focused on gaining the barkeeper's attention that she hadn't even noticed the man who had slipped in beside her. She looked him over quickly now. He wasn't particularly well-dressed, but he was clean and had a friendly smile, and that alone was enough right now. Perhaps he could be of some help.

"Good afternoon," she said as the door behind them opened and let in some much-needed daylight. "I'm Miss Montgomery. I don't suppose you know many people in this town?"

His smile grew broader, accentuating his bony cheeks. "Name's Roger. And I do know some folks. You planning to drink that?" He nodded at the glass in front of her.

"I most certainly am not, Mr. . . . . Roger."

He grinned again and reached for the glass. After downing the whiskey in one gulp, he asked, "Who are you looking for?"

Charlotte's hopes buoyed. "A woman by the name of Miss Lee. Ruby Lee. Although she may be Mrs. McNab by now. Her fiancé's name is Bertram McNab. They came here together from Baltimore a couple of months ago."

"McNab," the man repeated. It looked as if he was thinking, and so Charlotte waited, hoping he might have run into the Montgomery family's former maid and her fiancé—or husband.

"Yes. Mr. McNab was coming here to go into business with a friend. I don't know what sort of business, exactly, or the friend's name, but Ruby said the man was doing well." Charlotte paused, trying to remember the details of Mr. McNab's appearance from the one time she saw him paying a visit to Ruby in the Montgomerys' kitchen. "Mr. McNab is a tall man, dark hair. He has a winsome smile."

Roger wrinkled his forehead. "There are any number of men in town by that description. I can't say I've met him by name." He paused and took a small step closer to her. "But let me think a bit more."

The distance between them was less than polite—or comfortable—and Charlotte took a step backward. Roger chuckled.

"How old are you? Twenty? Twenty-two?" he asked, his eyes scrutinizing her face.

Before Charlotte could voice her indignation at his rude question, he continued on.

"And what's a sweet girl like you doing walking into a place like this?"

Charlotte's irritation rose like high tide back home, threatening to spill over. "I told you. I'm searching for someone. Now, do you know them or not?"

Apparently Roger found that question particularly funny, because he laughed. Then, in the blink of an eye, he'd stepped forward again and laid a hand over Charlotte's.

Charlotte yanked her hand away. "How dare—"

At that very second, another man shoved himself between her and Roger, placing his back firmly in front of Charlotte's face and forcing the offending man to stumble backward. She caught a whiff of tobacco and soap as she stepped around him.

"Leave the lady alone," the new man said in a low voice that left no room for questions or excuses.

The man was familiar. Charlotte tilted her head, her encounter with Roger all but forgotten as she took in this man's presence. Hair an unnameable shade between blond and brown, sharp green eyes, a face that was somehow both young and weathered, clean shaven, strong jaw, hands that were unmistakably strong...

She swallowed. It was the handsome but confused man from the depot. The one from whom she'd obtained the reference for a boarding house.

What was he doing *here*?

"Look now. You're interrupting a perfectly good conversation I was having—" Roger's voice went slightly shrill as he defended himself. And as much as Charlotte wished she could have slapped him across the face as she'd intended to do before this man stepped in, she had to admit she enjoyed the man looking cowed.

"That was no good conversation, and you know it," her rescuer fairly growled. He abruptly turned away from Roger, those green eyes landing on her. He extended an arm, as if he intended to escort her out of this place. "Come."

The word rankled Charlotte. She'd had more than enough of men telling her what to do, and despite the man's gallant actions, she was hardly about to follow his directives. She hadn't come all the way across the country on her own to be told what to do.

Instead, she fixed him with the strongest glare she could muster, turned on her heel, strode to the nearest empty table, and sat down.

Chapter Three

WHO *was* this woman?

Mark clenched his fists as she flounced into a chair, clearly showing no intentions of leaving this place. With a quick glare back at the weaselly man at the bar—who shrank back and held up his hands in surrender—Mark paced across the room to the table Miss Montgomery had chosen.

There was an empty chair across from her, but he didn't sit. "This isn't a place for a lady." He kept his words measured, his tone even. She couldn't suspect his interest in her was anything other than a gentleman's concern for a woman facing danger.

She narrowed her eyes at him. "I am perfectly capable of looking after myself, sir." She paused. "And how would you know I'm a lady?"

"Your clothing," he said. "And it didn't appear as if you were looking after yourself very well at all."

"I'll have you know that I was just about to slap that man across the face before you so rudely stepped in front of me. And if that hadn't stopped him, my brother showed me how to make a fist and punch a man if I ever needed to do so." She was entirely serious.

Mark actually found himself lost for words. The image of the well-dressed lady in front of him slamming a fist into that man's face played across his mind. He had absolutely no doubt she would have done it, too. Miss Charlotte Montgomery continued to be the exact opposite of everything he'd expected her to be.

Still, even if she hadn't needed his rescue, he had to convince her to leave this place. He couldn't fathom trying to explain to Chester Montgomery that his eldest daughter had gotten herself into a fight in a saloon.

"I don't suppose you're familiar with any other drinking establishments that I might visit?" she asked, making no move whatsoever to stand.

Mark blinked at her. For the love of all that was good, *what* was she thinking? Did she have some sort of predilection toward whiskey? He never would have thought—

"I do *not* imbibe." She stood now, giving him a withering look.

"I didn't think—" He paused. His goal here was twofold: first, to keep her safe, and second, to do so without her knowing who he was. "Forgive me. It's only that as a gentleman, I couldn't possibly live with myself if I thought you to be in any sort of trouble."

That seemed to soften her a bit. At least, she looked less likely to spew another set of barbed words at him.

Instead, she watched him a moment, as if she were assessing his worth. "I was told that the most likely place to find information about someone is a saloon."

That was intriguing. Chester Montgomery had indicated his daughter had run away for no reason whatsoever. "What sort of information are you trying to discover?" He paused, realizing that might seem too inquisitive for a man who was supposed to be a stranger. "I might be able to help."

She stood then, hope clearly blooming in her chocolate-colored eyes. "Are you from Cañon City, Mr. . . .?"

"Becker," he supplied. "Mark Becker. And yes, I've lived here." There was no need to detail that it was only for a few months here and there. His line of work tended to keep him moving from place to place.

"I'm Miss Montgomery." She kept her gaze pinned to him, and found himself growing somewhat uncomfortable with her perusal. Miss Charlotte Montgomery was bolder than half the men Mark knew. "I'm looking for a woman I knew back in Maryland. A Miss Ruby Lee, and her fiancé—or potentially her husband—a Mr. Bertram McNab."

The names were unfamiliar to Mark, and he resolved to inquire about them to Mr. Montgomery's man as soon as he had a free moment to make his way to the telegraph office. But right now he had to figure out how to keep Miss Montgomery from striding off to the next saloon.

"I'm afraid I don't know either of them. But perhaps a visit to the boarding houses and hotels in town might be more fruitful? Or the general stores and mercantiles?" He held his breath as she considered his words.

"Yes," she finally said. "I believe you may be right. Neither Miss Lee nor her intended are given to drink, and they must have a place to stay and a place where they can purchase their sundries. Thank you, Mr. Becker. You've been most helpful."

She moved past him then, toward the door of the saloon. She was fast, and was already outside before he caught up with her.

"Please," he said, glancing around them as the shadows of dusk had begun to appear. "Let me accompany you back to your boarding house. It's growing dark, and it isn't safe for a lady alone at night."

"I appreciate the gallantry, but I'm perfectly capable of walking myself. Particularly when it's hardly dark at all. Good night, Mr. Becker." She began walking down the plank sidewalk, her reticule clutched to her side and her hand grasping the narrow brim of her hat as a gust of wind kicked up. He clenched his hands to his sides. She was *not* going to be an easy one to keep out of trouble.

She paused and turned, and for a half a moment, Mark thought she'd reconsidered his offer. Perhaps she wasn't as hard-headed as she appeared.

"I failed to thank you for your efforts on my behalf in that establishment," she said. "Although I didn't particularly need saving, I do thank you."

And with that, she was off again, leaving Mark standing in front of the saloon. One thing was for certain—he would be earning every penny Montgomery paid him.

Chapter Four

NEITHER OF THE TWO hotels closest to Charlotte's boarding house had Ruby or her intended on their guest lists. And a visit to the boarding house two streets over had yielded no results either. There were a couple of other boarding houses she could visit—"less reputable" ones, as one of the hotel clerks had described them. But Charlotte thought she might stop in to some of the shops first.

She would never admit it out loud, but the incident with that man at the saloon the night before had shaken her. But only a little, and only because the entire experience had been unexpected. Cañon City was not Baltimore, and even then, it wasn't as if she'd spent time in the less savory parts of the city. She need only keep her wits about her, and she'd be just fine.

Charlotte pressed open the door to the shop with the sign that read *Hill's General Store*. Inside, a nice array of goods met her eyes. Charlotte smiled at it all. She so loved it here. Everything was just barely on the edge of civilized. This store, for instance. It was lovely and inviting, and yet right outside the door, one could run into any number of disreputable people. Like that man at the saloon.

Her father would despise this place, and everyone and everything in it. Which made it exactly what she'd hoped it would be.

She decided she liked this little shop most of all, with its carefully arranged merchandise and the kindly older woman smiling at her from behind the counter that ran along the wall to the left.

"Do you need help, dear?" the woman asked in a voice that reminded Charlotte of a particularly wonderful nanny she'd had as a child.

Charlotte returned the woman's smile as she made her way to the counter. "Yes, I'm hoping you might answer a question for me." She stopped at the counter. "You have a lovely shop."

"Thank you." The woman beamed. "It's my son's. I enjoy helping the customers. His wife has a dress shop in the back. Did you see it? She's quite talented."

Charlotte turned to look toward where the woman pointed. Shelving blocked most of the view, but she could just make out a door that must have led to the dress shop.

"I'm Mrs. Hill," the woman said, drawing Charlotte's attention back to the counter. "Now, tell me your question and I'll see if I can help."

Charlotte quickly introduced herself, and then asked if Mrs. Hill had seen either Ruby or her fiancé.

Mrs. Hill thought for a moment. "I'm sorry, dear. I can't say that I'm familiar with either of them. Of course, we get a lot of new folks in here, and I don't always catch their names. Is it terribly important? I can ask my son when he returns."

Charlotte drew in a disappointed breath. "That would be wonderful. Thank you for all of your help. I'll stop by again later." She paused. "You don't happen to carry lavender soap, do you? It's my favorite, and I fear I didn't leave room in my bag for it when I left home."

"We do, indeed. I'll set some aside for you, if you like."

"Thank you. I'll return this evening." Charlotte bade Mrs. Hill goodbye, and left through the front door.

Outside, the sun shone brightly above, warming the day. Charlotte hadn't expected it to be so chilly in June, particularly in the mornings and evenings. She'd brought a wrap, but not a coat, and the warmth of the sun made her tilt her face up to better feel its warmth on her face.

She began walking slowly down the road, with no particular destination in mind. Perhaps she would run across another of the town's general stores. She hadn't expected Ruby to be this difficult to find. It didn't matter, really, whether Charlotte found her. She'd simply hoped to find a familiar face so far from home. It wasn't as if Ruby were expecting her.

But now that the former maid had become so hard to locate, Charlotte couldn't ignore the worry that curled up from her stomach. What if something terrible had befallen Ruby and her Mr. McNab?

She shook her head. It was unlikely. If anything, they'd simply decided that the opportunity in Cañon City wasn't as they'd expected, and they'd gone elsewhere.

She'd continue asking around for Ruby, at least to the other boarding houses and general stores. And if that didn't work, she'd resign herself to her own company. As nice as it would be to have a friend here, ultimately it wasn't necessary for Charlotte to accomplish what she came here to do. And that was simply to wait out her father's insistence on her marriage to a man of his choosing.

Charlotte shuddered, drawing the wrap even tighter around her despite the sun, as she thought of the odious Mr.

Lindstrom. He was more than twice her age, with a bulbous nose and a leering gaze. All Papa saw was wealth and position, and he'd refused to hear her objections over the match. Mama heard them but refused to go against Papa's wishes.

And so Charlotte had left.

Ruby had told Charlotte of Mr. McNab's prospects here before she'd left with him, just a couple of months before Charlotte herself had boarded a train west. She could have gone anywhere, and she would have, if necessary. But why not choose a town that housed at least one person she knew? She'd never imagined it would be this difficult to find Ruby, though.

She happened upon another general store, this one on the far side of town, and stepped inside just as another gust of wind rustled her skirts. This store wasn't as comforting or as prettily laid out as Hill's General Store, but it still displayed a good array of items for purchase. Charlotte surmised it was Mrs. Hill's touch that had made the other store so much more inviting.

She made her way to the counter and asked the proprietor the question she'd posed at the lodging establishments and Hill's General Store.

"Smaller woman?" the man asked, holding his hand out to indicate a lady of a height much shorter than Charlotte's own stature. "Light colored hair?"

Hope blossomed in Charlotte's heart. "Yes! You've seen her?"

The store owner shrugged. "It may be. This lady was in here just last week. I only remember her because she signed her name McNab, and my sister married a McNab up in Colorado City." He reached for an open ledger that sat on the counter and flipped back a couple of pages. "Here."

Charlotte looked to the line where he pointed. There, in neat script, it read, *Mrs. Bertram McNab, Riverside Boarding House*, with an amount due.

It was Ruby. It *had* to be. "Thank you so very much," she said, looking up at the proprietor. "I believe this is the woman for whom I'm searching. Now, I don't suppose you have any lengths of ribbon in stock?"

She ought to have asked for something else, Charlotte realized as the man fetched and proudly held out two very old, very sad-looking spools of dun and gray ribbon. Oh well, it was money well-spent if it meant she could find Ruby.

As the proprietor cut and wrapped the ribbon for her, she inquired after the whereabouts of the Riverside Boarding House.

"I don't know why they named it such, but it's nowhere near the river," he said. He told her where to find it, pressed the wrapped package across the counter toward her, and leveled a serious gaze. "If I were you, I wouldn't visit there alone. It isn't the most reputable of places."

Charlotte swallowed as concern for Ruby flared yet again deep down inside. "Thank you, sir. I do appreciate it. I'll be cautious."

He nodded, and she tucked the package between her arm and her side as she left the shop.

Outside, she paused, considering her options. It was broad daylight, hardly the time in which menacing folk were about. But who knew what she could find inside a boarding house?

She adjusted her gloves as she thought, her eyes traveling the street toward the location of the boarding house. A quick movement near the doorway of a nearby store caught her eye.

If she wasn't mistaken, that was a man who had slipped quickly inside. A man with scuffed boots and a brown hat.

Mr. Becker.

It *was* awfully curious that she'd run into him so frequently. After all, the town was sizable enough that it hadn't happened with anyone else she'd met since arriving. Not even with the man in the long coat her father had clearly hired to follow her on her journey west.

She'd figured that out almost immediately, after she'd caught the fellow looking at her more than once, and not with anything one could consider admiration or curiosity. His neat dress—and frequent passes by her seat—made his occupation even more evident. He hadn't interrupted her, and as far as she was concerned, he could notify her father that she was happy, confident, and determined all he liked so long as he didn't impede her progress.

Charlotte had been certain Papa would keep him employed once she'd reached town, and yet she hadn't seen him once.

But she *had* seen Mr. Becker frequently, with his devilishly handsome grin and his penchant for lurking just where she might need him.

Her brow furrowed as she considered the shop where she'd seen him disappear. A slight smile lifting the corner of her mouth, she made a decision.

She strolled directly past the shop to walk toward the Riverside Boarding House.

And she'd see if Mr. Mark Becker might find her there.

Chapter Five

THIS WOMAN WAS GOING to be the death of him.

Why could she simply be content with visiting other ladies at the boarding house, or, better yet, keeping to her room? Instead, here she was again, traipsing about town, and this time headed into an area she ought to avoid—if she had a modicum of sense in her head.

And yet, as he peered around the corner of a building, Mark had to acknowledge a grudging respect for Miss Montgomery. She clearly hadn't a shred of fear in her body, and she approached everyone she met as an equal despite the fact that her father made more money in a day than most men made in a year.

She paused outside a nondescript building. From this angle, Mark couldn't tell if it was the boarding house or the neighboring saloon. Surely she'd had her fill of saloons last night, and considering she'd taken to heart his suggestion to visit general stores and boarding houses, he supposed the saloon wasn't what had her so intrigued.

Thankfully.

Miss Montgomery slipped inside the building, and after a heartbeat, Mark stepped around the corner and made his way down the road to the boarding house. He paused outside, his heart sinking when he saw the place.

He hadn't been in this area recently, and what used to be an inexpensive but clean establishment looked as if it had devolved into something much worse. The exterior of the building was so unkempt, with boards over one window and a broken sign, that he feared what the inside would contain. Or *who* it might contain.

The door opened, and he stepped back, only to find himself under the scrutiny of a man missing one eye and sporting a black bruise around the other. On his arm was a woman Mark immediately knew wasn't the man's wife, not with the gaudy skirts and the way she eyed him as if he were her next meal.

And Miss Montgomery had gone into this place *alone*.

Mark didn't wait another second. All thoughts of remaining unseen and ensuring her safety from a distance fled his mind as he threw open the door. If she was in here and being hurt or manhandled in any way—

He ran straight into a person. And not just any person . . .

Mark reached up and grabbed onto Miss Montgomery's arms to keep her from falling backward. "I apologize. Are you all right?"

She straightened and looked down at his hands which were still clamped around her arms. Mark yanked them away and shoved his hands into his trousers pockets. If he wasn't mistaken, a pink flush had crept into Miss Montgomery's cheeks. But the lighting was hardly decent in here, with one remaining dirty window providing the only light to speak of. Still, the idea of his hands on her arms making her flush was . . .

Stupid. It was irresponsible and very, very *stupid*. And if there was one thing Mark was, it was smart. Smart enough not to even let himself entertain the thoughts that had just run through his mind.

Miss Montgomery crossed her arms, a package tucked underneath one, and narrowed her eyes. Any trace of a blush that might have existed now gone completely. "Why are you here?"

"I'm looking for someone." It was hardly a lie; after all, he was looking for *her*.

"Mmm," she said.

He adjusted his jacket, although it needed no adjusting. "May I ask why you've come to such a place?"

"You were the one who suggested I ask around at boarding houses." Her words were cutting, and it took all his self-control not to wince.

"Yes," he said in an even voice. "Although I meant *reputable* places. This one is hardly . . ." He trailed off as the front door opened to admit a fellow who careened sideways and reeked of whiskey.

The man paused and leaned a hand against the wall while his eyes found Miss Montgomery. Mark bit his tongue for a moment. But the man's unabashed perusal remained transfixed upon Miss Montgomery.

"Move along," he snarled at the drunken fellow. The man lurched for the nearby stairs and disappeared up into the darkness.

"As I said," he continued. "Hardly reputable. Your friend wouldn't find this establishment up to her standards."

Miss Montgomery had uncrossed her arms, but at his words, she raised her eyebrows. "And how would you know what Miss Lee's standards might be?"

"I presume they'd be akin to your own. Or higher, given your preclusion to visiting saloons." It was his irritation at having to yank her out of situations she ought not have found herself in that made him say that last bit out loud, but she didn't grow angry with him.

Instead, she laughed.

"You'll find I'm not your average lady, Mr. Becker," she said, a smile still on her face. "I'm not given to fits of the vapors, and I never shirk a challenge."

"I can see that," he said dryly. "Now, may I escort you out of this establishment?" He offered an arm, but she took a step backward.

"Not until I ask after Miss Lee. Or Mrs. McNab, as I found out at one of the general stores. Besides, I thought you were searching for someone also?" She raised those eyebrows again, appearing to question everything about him.

"Yes. By all means." He gestured toward the hallway, indicating she ought to go first. Who knew where they might find the proprietor of this place, given the man was disinclined to meet folks at the door.

"Somehow, Mr. Becker," she said as she passed him, those luminous brown eyes holding his gaze, "I believe you might have been searching for me."

His blood thrummed in his ears as he followed her down the hallway. Had she figured him out? He silently cursed Mr. Montgomery. It was impossible to keep this girl out of trouble without intervening. If she'd figured him out, it would be no wonder.

The hallway led to a kitchen that ran along the rear of the building. The cook glared at them when the entered through the door.

"No guests in the kitchen." She pointed with a long spoon at the door, indicating they ought to turn right back around and leave.

"We aren't guests," Miss Montgomery said. "I'm hoping you might tell me where to find the proprietor of this boarding house?"

"Hallway. First door on the right. Salt!" The cook barked the order at a scrawny kitchen maid who stood timidly nearby.

Miss Montgomery hurriedly thanked the woman and slipped through the door Mark opened. She walked immediately to the door the cook had indicated in the hallway and knocked insistently. Uncertain who might actually answer the door, Mark gently took her wrist and pulled her to the side while he took her place.

And surprisingly, she not only let him, but she did so without glaring at him.

A scruffy-looking older man answered, pulling the door open just far enough to let them see his face. "You and the missus looking for a room?"

"Uh . . . no," he said, momentarily caught off guard with the man's assumption that he and Miss Montgomery were husband and wife. He glanced at Miss Montgomery, whose face had gone pink again. If it was in reaction to the indication that they were married, he dared not think on it too long.

"We're looking for friends who may have taken a room here. McNab is the last name, a man and a woman," he continued.

"Mr. Bertram McNab," Miss Montgomery supplied.

"McNab," the owner repeated. His face pulled into a frown. "They stayed here, for a while. Left to go to their own place." He lifted his hand and pointed a finger at them. "You see Mc-Nab, you tell him he still owes me for their last week here. I never should've let him go without it. Slippery-tongued, that one is."

"I will," Miss Montgomery said carefully as Mark turned the man's words over in his mind. Who precisely *were* these people for whom Miss Montgomery was searching? They were not, as he'd originally presumed, some society miss and her opportunity-minded husband.

"Did Mr. McNab say where their new home is?" Miss Montgomery asked the proprietor.

He shook his head. "Didn't ask. But I'd like to lay eyes on the coins he owes me. You tell him that."

After Miss Montgomery again promised to do just that, Mark thanked the man and ushered her out of that place as quickly as possible.

Outside, he grabbed hold of her arm, intending to demand to know who these McNabs were, but she spoke first, shaking off his grasp.

"Now, Mr. Becker, will you tell me how much my father is paying you to follow me around town?"

Chapter Six

MR. BECKER'S FACE WENT from surprised to irritated to amused all within the span of three seconds.

"More than I've made at any job I've had in my life." He paused. "You weren't supposed to know."

At least he didn't try to deny it. Charlotte appreciated that immeasurably. "My father consistently underestimates my intellect. I'm thankful it appears that you don't also."

He took off his hat and ran a hand over his dark blond hair. Strands of it caught the light from the sun. He must spend a lot of time outside, considering how that same sun had tanned his skin. And then the way the line of his jaw—

What was she thinking? Charlotte swallowed, trying to get hold of her runaway thoughts. This man was being *paid* to follow her. And an exorbitant sum too, if she knew her father. She ought to be angry at the both of them.

But Mr. Becker looked somehow both sheepish and determined, as if he was embarrassed he'd been caught and yet wasn't about to give up the work either. It was admirable, she thought.

"Miss Montgomery, I—"

"I won't tell him," she said suddenly. "My father, I mean. I'd hate to put you out of work. Besides, you've done well at it. Aside from letting me figure it all out, anyhow."

One corner of his lips lifted in an irritated smirk. "It's difficult to remain unseen when one must constantly jump to your rescue."

"I didn't ask for help," she reminded him. He did that all on his own. "My father said nothing to you about returning me to Baltimore?"

He shook his head. "My only instructions are to ensure your safety."

That was interesting. Perhaps Papa thought she'd grow tired of Colorado and return on her own to beg forgiveness and marry Mr. Lindstrom. Well, that would certainly never happen. She'd stay here until she was old and gray before she married that man.

Mr. Becker was watching her with a curious expression, as if he wished to know her thoughts. And suddenly, she wanted him to know she was more than some disobedient, wealthy girl.

"It was an arranged marriage," she said quickly, looking out across the road as she spoke. "My father wishes me to marry a man more than twice my age for money and for the connections it will bring him. I doubt he told you. But that's why I'm here."

She drew her gaze back to Mr. Becker. Those green eyes held hers, and his expression was unreadable. Finally, he nodded, although he said nothing.

Perhaps she ought not have told him. Feeling a bit silly, Charlotte looked down and occupied herself with rearranging the package of ribbon under her arm. He either didn't care one way or the other, or he agreed with her father.

"I plan to return home once he agrees to let me choose who I marry," she added quietly, more to remind herself than give Mr. Becker the information.

Mr. Becker didn't react to those words either. Instead, he extended an arm. "May I escort you back to your boarding house? If you say no, I regret to inform you that I'll be following from a distance anyhow."

The hint of a smile twitched his lips on an otherwise serious expression, and Charlotte found herself laughing. "All right. I suppose you may."

When she crooked her arm around his, he tucked her elbow securely against him. It was a protective gesture, one more suited for a courting pair than for two people who were essentially strangers to each other. Part of Charlotte wanted to yank her arm away and decree her independence. Yet the other part reveled in his nearness.

Her face went warm at the last thought. What was wrong with her? Mr. Becker was a man hired by her father to do exactly this. As much as she might admire the way his hair fell from under his hat or how broad his shoulders were or the low growl of his voice when he spoke with any man he thought was a threat, she'd be a fool to give in to those sorts of feelings.

"Tell me," she said in a tone she hoped was light and didn't convey anything that was truly running through her mind. "How did my father find you?"

"Gold," he replied.

"I'm sorry?" Charlotte glanced up at him, but his eyes were on everything that was around them.

"I worked a while for the Granger Stage Line Company on their runs out of gold country," he said. "They paid well for any man brave enough—or foolish enough—to ride shotgun messenger out of those towns. Mr. Montgomery found one of my associates, who recommended me."

"That sounds like dangerous work." Charlotte tried and failed to imagine what it must have been like.

"It was that." His eyes, darkened like the color of moss in the shade, found hers.

She swallowed, suddenly thankful he'd survived it to be here now. "Why did you leave it?"

"I'd had enough of being shot. Men get desperate when wealth is at stake."

"You were shot?" Her eyes widened at the thought. No wonder he'd left that job.

"Twice," he said with a wince. "You'd think once would be enough, but I was hard-headed enough to go back for a second one."

She smiled at the self-deprecation. "Well, I'm glad the bullets were not life-threatening."

"Or else I wouldn't be here now, following you about town?"

Charlotte laughed. "Precisely." She paused outside a photography studio as an idea blossomed. "Would you be opposed to helping me? Considering I imagine you must continue tracing my every step?"

His mouth lifted in a half-smile, and Charlotte's breath caught in her throat. Why, of all things, did Mr. Becker have to be so handsome? Couldn't her father have hired a gargoyle of a man instead?

He considered her for a moment, and just as Charlotte thought she might explode from the waiting, he nodded. "I don't see why not. After all, the sooner you locate your friend, the sooner you'll stop gallivanting around town."

"Hmm. Well, thank you." She began to move forward again, a smile playing upon her lips.

Mr. Becker took a large stride so as not to lose hold of her elbow. "You will, right? Quit visiting saloons and shadowy boarding houses?" He asked the questions as if he expected her to ride half-dressed down Main Street next.

Charlotte gave him a mischievous grin. It was far too much to let him relax just yet. "Perhaps."

"Perhaps," he repeated, his voice on the edge of exasperated. He shook his head. "Ought to have taken that position guarding the prison instead."

And Charlotte laughed. Somehow, with Mr. Becker at her side, her worries felt less troublesome. He'd help her find Ruby, she'd while away her time in Cañon City in a pleasant manner, and then, she'd return home when her father relented.

Something about that last thought didn't spark as much hope as it normally did, and Charlotte frowned for a moment. But it was too nice a day, and Mr. Becker's smile was far too friendly, and this town was much too interesting for the questionable feeling to remain for long.

Chapter Seven

RUBY MCNAB MUST HAVE disappeared from town like a ghost. Or so that was all Mark could figure had happened. No one else he asked seemed to have heard of the woman or her new husband.

As he walked toward Miss Montgomery's boarding house—where she'd promised she'd stay put for once—he turned what they knew over in his mind. Only the general store owner and the boarding house proprietor had known of Mrs. McNab. Either she and her new husband were deliberately hiding—which seemed unlikely—or they'd left town. Otherwise *someone* should have known where they currently resided.

Just a few doors from the boarding house sat a small restaurant. The place looked busy, a sure sign the food was good.

Mark still thought of the restaurant when he arrived at the boarding house, where Miss Montgomery sat impatiently perched on the edge of a chair in the parlor.

He shook his head immediately, and Miss Montgomery's hopeful smile dropped. But she quickly recovered and stood, walking toward him with her dark hair arranged in a cascade of curls that framed her face.

"Are you hungry?" he asked before he lost his nerve. "I saw a restaurant just down the road that looked good."

Miss Montgomery raised her eyebrows. She was either horrified or surprised at his question, and Mark began to wonder if he should have kept the idea to himself. He could only imagine what Chester Montgomery would think of this situation. Just as he was about to retract the question, Miss Montgomery rewarded him with a smile.

"That would be lovely," she said as she clasped her hands together. "I was just beginning to think of lunch. Perhaps you can tell me more about what you found, or didn't find, that is."

And then, before he knew it, Mark found himself arm in arm with Miss Montgomery as they strolled down the road toward the restaurant, trying not to think of how she smelled of lavender and how pretty her smile was when she shot one his way.

They were seated at a cozy little table by the window. After they each ordered the roast chicken dish, Mark told Miss Montgomery about who he had spoken with and what he hadn't been able to find.

"I fear they may have left town," he finished.

Miss Montgomery glanced out the window, a pensive expression fixed to her lips. When she turned back to Mark, she said, "Well, I appreciate you asking around for me. I wish I could've found Ruby, but I suppose it doesn't particularly matter one way or the other."

"She wasn't expecting you?' It was a question Mark had wondered since Miss Montgomery had first mentioned her friend.

"Oh no," she said. "Ruby was one of our kitchen maids. We had something of a friendship back at home."

The pieces of the puzzle fell together. A kitchen maid. That made so much more sense than the well-to-do lady Mark had assumed Mrs. McNab to be.

"I know it's an odd sort of friendship," Miss Montgomery continued. "However when one finds oneself bored to tears on a Saturday afternoon, entertainment can always be found in the kitchen. Ruby tried to teach me all sorts of things—baking bread, mixing up cakes, even cooking chicken like this." She pointed at their plates, which had just arrived.

"Tried?" Mark paused, his fork hovering over his plate.

Miss Montgomery laughed, and it reminded him of church bells on Christmas Eve. The sound brought a smile to his face as he speared a piece of chicken.

"I must admit that I never quite mastered any of it," Miss Montgomery replied. "It's a good thing I haven't needed to cook for myself here. I'm afraid I might starve."

"Surely it can't be that bad. It can't be worse than my attempts at beans," Mark said.

"Oh no, my creations are truly terrible. You may break your teeth."

Mark laughed.

"Thankfully, I never had to cook to survive," she said as she set her fork down.

Mark thought back to when his mother patiently taught his younger sister how to knead bread and cut carrots. And then he tried to imagine being wealthy enough that such skills weren't needed. "Did your parents discover your friendship with Mrs. McNab?"

Miss Montgomery appeared to think for a moment as she rested her fork on her plate. "They didn't. I was forever disappointing them, so I doubt they would have been surprised."

She glanced at him with an expression so heartbreaking that Mark reached out and laid his hand upon hers. He hadn't fully realized what he'd done right away, thinking only that she was hurting and he wished to comfort her. And once he did realize that this might not be the wisest decision, he didn't much want to pull his hand away.

Charlotte's eyes darted to their hands, but she made no move to extract hers. Mark's heart swelled with some undefinable hope as he kept his palm resting over the back of her smaller hand.

"I don't see how you could be a disappointment to anyone, much less your parents," he finally said, dragging his mind back to the conversation.

She gave him the ghost of a smile. "When I was young, I was forever climbing trees and tearing my stockings. I much preferred conversing with the gardener or the cook to perfecting my needlepoint or sitting quietly. I even convinced Anthony—that's my oldest brother—to show me how to fight when I was twelve. But now . . . mostly my mother worries about how brash I am with company and how little I'm interested in meeting the men my father carefully chooses. Such as Mr. Lindstrom." She shuddered slightly at the name.

A flicker of irritation at his employer sparked inside of Mark at Miss Montgomery's words. What sort of man wanted to push his daughter into a marriage that would surely be unhappy?

A man who was paying him, that's who.

But here, with Miss Montgomery sitting across from him looking every bit of the vulnerable yet confident woman she was, Mark wondered if the money was worth her misery.

He tightened his hand around hers. He shouldn't feel guilty. After all, it wasn't as if Mr. Montgomery had asked him to push Miss Montgomery into marriage. He only needed to keep her safe.

"Are you all right?" Miss Montgomery's voice was laced with a quiet concern. "It looks as if something is troubling you."

Had he been that obvious with his thoughts? The idea sat uneasily with him. What if Miss Montgomery could see the effect she was beginning to have on him?

Mark quickly arranged his face into a neutral expression. "I'm fine. I only wish I could have helped you find Mrs. Mc-Nab."

"Are you speaking of Ruby McNab?" Their waitress, a tall, slim woman older than both Mark and Miss Montgomery, had returned with a pitcher of water. Mark yanked his hand away, stowing it safely on his lap.

"Yes, indeed, we are." Miss Montgomery turned her friendly smile to the waitress. "Do you know her?"

The waitress refilled each of their water glasses before speaking. She clutched the pitcher between both hands. "I'm afraid to say I did know her. She worked here for a while. Hired her on myself. I thought she was a nice girl, newly married and needing to earn some money."

The waitress frowned. "I didn't realize that her idea of earning money was stealing everything we had made in a week."

Chapter Eight

RUBY, A THIEF? CHARLOTTE couldn't possibly believe it.

At the restaurant, she barely tasted the remainder of her meal as she turned the waitress's words over in her head. And as they walked back to her boarding house, she began to wonder at the possibility of the woman's words being true. Mark reassured her that they'd find out for certain, that it could all be a misunderstanding. How they'd find out whether or not it was true, Charlotte didn't know, especially since no one in town could point them toward where Ruby lived—or could even tell them if she was still in Cañon City.

The next morning, she awoke not with Ruby or what still awaited her back in Baltimore on her mind. Instead, she sat up with a start, rubbing her eyes as if that could erase the embarrassing dream she'd just had. When that didn't work, she stood and splashed water from the nearby basin onto her face.

Charlotte blinked at herself in the small mirror that sat atop the spindly dressing table. Her eyes were wide and her hair a wild mess, even as droplets of water dripped down her face. She laughed at herself and sank into the chair that sat in front of the dressing table.

As much as she often acted on impulse, Charlotte considered herself a reasonably sensible woman. For instance, most girls in her position would have acquiesced to her father's request. But all Charlotte could see was a lifetime of misery, and so, very sensibly, she thought, she said no and came here.

Where she now spent her days—and apparently her dreams too—with the devilishly handsome Mark Becker.

She grabbed a brush and began to tame her hair. It was far less embarrassing to think about hairstyle than to relive that dream kiss. She needed to push *that* from her mind before she met with him today, or else she'd probably blush scarlet the moment she laid eyes upon him.

But it was no use.

Mr. Becker was waiting for her in the parlor when she finished breakfast. He gave her an easy smile, and Charlotte's face went warmer than the sun on an August day in Maryland. But, gentleman that he was, he said not a word about it, even though she was almost certain he could read the thoughts that went through her mind.

She needed to get a hold of herself. Because truth be told, she didn't necessarily *mind* remembering that dream.

"I thought we might speak with the sheriff," he said.

Charlotte nodded, not entirely trusting herself to speak. His eyes were particularly green today, and had she noticed the way his hair curled just slightly at the nape of his neck? She looked down, which seemed much safer than looking *at* him any longer—at least until she could come to her senses again.

"I've not met him, but I've heard Sheriff Young is—" He stopped mid-sentence as a young man entered the boarding house.

The newcomer came immediately to Charlotte. "I've the mail for the ladies here," he said as he held out a stack of envelopes and a small parcel tied with string.

"I can take it," she said. "Thank you."

Blessedly, Mr. Becker had a coin in his pocket that he handed the boy. Charlotte crossed the room to the little desk that sat just outside the parlor near the front door. Grateful for the distraction from Mr. Becker's broad shoulders and the way the corners of his eyes crinkled when he smiled, she sat the envelopes and parcel on the desk.

The topmost envelope caught her eye. It was addressed to *Miss Charlotte Montgomery* in a light, swoopy script that Charlotte immediately recognized.

Mama.

Charlotte collected the letter with fingers that trembled just slightly. Of course Mr. Becker would have had to inform her father about where she was staying. She couldn't blame him for that. After all, he was only doing his job.

But she hadn't expected either of her parents to reach out to her so soon.

Clutching the envelope in her hand, she returned to the parlor where Mr. Becker waited.

"Are you well?" He looked at her with concern tracing his features. And all Charlotte could think was that at least the presence of the envelope had caused her mind to right itself in regards to him.

"Yes," she finally said before showing him the envelope. "It's from my mother."

Ever the gentleman, he gestured at the nearest seat, a chair with a straight back and a red upholstered cushion on the seat.

Charlotte sank gratefully onto the chair. Then she drew in her breath, pressed her shoulders back, and slid her finger under the lip of the envelope to open it. It was best to get the reading of it over with. At least then she'd know whether to pack her bags and leave—whether to Baltimore or elsewhere—or remain where she was.

Mr. Becker occupied himself with examining the paltry décor on the fireplace mantel while Charlotte read. The letter was short and to-the-point.

My Dearest Charlotte,

I write to you to persuade you to come to your senses and return home. Mary and I worry about you daily. Poor Mr. Lindstrom is beside himself. He fears for your safety. Dear Charlotte, he yearns to marry you. I only ask that you thoroughly consider how good this marriage would be for you. Mr. Lindstrom is a fine man with many good qualities. Your father would not have considered him otherwise.

It is time you gave up these childish antics and realized what is best for you. You must give consideration to your sister, too. Your behavior could prevent Mary from finding a suitable match when it is her time. Please reply and let me know when we might expect your return.

All my love,

Mama

A gush of air escaped Charlotte's lips as the paper crumpled between her fingers. What was best for her? It was more like what was best for her father. And how good could a marriage be when she held no attraction or affection for the man she married? Despite her mother's words, she doubted Mary blamed her much at all for leaving.

"It doesn't look as if you've received good news." Mr. Becker had returned to stand beside her.

Charlotte mutely held out the letter. He took it and made quick work of the reading.

"Hmm," was all he said.

A million feelings rushed through her all at once, and she stood, trying to make sense of them all. "Childish antics! I should have known they wouldn't have seen it any other way. And if Mr. Lindstrom is truly concerned for me, he'd realize I have no interest in him and he would rescind his proposal." She stalked across the room, looked out the window without really seeing, and then strode back.

Mr. Becker still held the letter. He turned it over in his hand and then looked up at her.

"Would you like me to toss it into the fire?" He gestured at the fireplace, which held a low-burning fire to ward off the morning's chill.

"The fire?" Charlotte was certain her jaw had dropped open at the unusual suggestion. "Whatever for?"

Mr. Becker shrugged. "Well, if I received a missive that made me as angry as this one has made you, I'd derive a good amount of satisfaction over watching it burn."

If Charlotte hadn't been so angry, she would have laughed. Still, his suggestion had cooled some of the rage she'd felt. It melted now into a giant sense of disappointment.

"No, that's quite all right." She held out her hand and he returned the letter. But what *would* she do with it?

Without thinking, she moved toward the fireplace and dropped it into the flames. They made quick work of the paper, and when Charlotte turned, she found Mr. Becker next to her, watching her with a satisfactory look lingering on his lips.

"It feels better, right?" he asked.

"I suppose, in a way. I just . . ." She threw up her hands. "I don't know what I'm supposed to do now. I came all the way here, certain that it would cause Papa to relent. But it hasn't—and now it appears he won't. My grand plan has failed. What do I do now?"

"Well . . ." Mr. Becker tucked his hands into his pockets and leaned against the mantel. "I imagine you could do anything you want."

Charlotte swallowed. Could she? It seemed an impossible sort of suggestion, like thinking that one could simply stop blinking or breathing air. "What would you do if you were in my position?"

"I suppose I'd seek out work looking after wayward heiresses."

Charlotte burst into laughter. "I suppose you would." She glanced again into the fire, where all traces of her mother's writing were now gone. "I never imagined being away from my family. As much as they irritate me at times, I always thought I'd be with them, or at least nearby."

"It isn't easy," Mr. Becker said. "Not a day goes by that I don't think about my parents or my siblings. But the pain lessens some as time goes on."

Charlotte drew in a deep breath, turning his words over in her mind. "It makes sense, but . . ." Her throat seemed to close as unshed tears pricked at her eyes. "I miss them, my sister and my brothers. And my parents . . . I miss them too, but I suppose I miss who I wish they were more than who they actually are."

Her body shook just slightly. Charlotte wrapped her arms around herself, trying to hold it in, but it was too late. Mr. Becker had already taken notice and stepped forward. Before she knew it, he'd enveloped her in his arms.

"Charlotte," he said, his voice barely a whisper. "It will all be well. I promise."

His words seemed to burrow straight into her soul. She sunk into his reassuring embrace, letting her arms drop to her sides, and, for once, allowing herself to mourn what she'd wanted most in her entire life. Her parents would never accept her for the way she was, and there was no doing anything about that.

As a few tears leaked from her eyes into Mr. Becker's shirt, Charlotte let all of her expectations go. She forgot her parents. She forgot the rigid rules of Baltimore society. She forgot what everyone assumed she needed to be. She forgot that Mr. Becker oughtn't call her *Charlotte*. She forgot that anyone could walk in at any moment to catch them in this compromising position.

Instead, she breathed in his scent, a mix of tobacco and soap, and reveled in the warm strength of his embrace. And she felt that perhaps he was right.

Maybe she could do anything she wanted.

Chapter Nine

"BERTRAM MCNAB'S WIFE?" Sheriff Ben Young rubbed a hand over the back of his neck.

"Yes, I believe so. That's what the woman at the restaurant said," Mark replied. He shifted to avoid the blinding sun coming through the front window of the sheriff's office.

The sheriff nodded. "I remember now. That happened right about the same time as McNab found himself in a spot of trouble with a few of the business owners in town. Seemed he liked to purchase on credit—except he never paid the credit down. They skipped town right after I heard about Mrs. McNab making off with money from Mrs. Smith's place."

It was probably best that they were long gone. Charlotte would be disappointed, but it didn't sound as if this friend of hers was much worth knowing these days.

He thanked the sheriff as he mentally chastised himself for thinking of her as *Charlotte* again. He'd made a mistake caving into that desire to be familiar with her yesterday. If her father had any idea, he'd not only be out of work in an instant, he'd likely find his name smeared from here to San Francisco.

And yet, how could it be a mistake if it felt so *right*?

Outside, he drew in a great gulp of air to help set his mind straight. Charlotte ought to be back at the boarding house by this hour. He'd extracted a promise from her not to pay a visit to any place remotely scandalous while he attended to meeting with the sheriff and penning a report to Mr. Montgomery. She claimed she would only while away her day at Grace Hill's dress shop and perhaps a hat shop. When he asked if she needed money, she laughed and informed him that although she didn't bring much from home, money was the one thing she hadn't left behind.

The memory drew a smile to his face as he approached the boarding house. The more he got to know Charlotte, the more he understood how exceedingly sensible she was. And like the rest of her, that was unexpected.

Although, he realized, by this point, nothing should surprise him about Charlotte Montgomery.

"Is Miss Montgomery in?" he asked the friendly older woman at the desk just inside the door of the boarding house.

"No, sir." She gave a shake of her head as she tapped a short pencil against her ledger book. "Miss Montgomery hasn't returned yet."

Mark turned the brim of his hat around in his hands. How long could it possibly take a woman to purchase a dress?

The woman behind the desk must have noticed his perplexed expression, because she smiled at him. "You must have been the one she waited on." When he said nothing, she added, "When she returned from her shopping, she waited down here for a while and then told me she was going to take a walk down by the river. I imagine that's where she still is, unless she's gotten hungry."

Mark thanked the woman and tugged his hat back onto his head. It wasn't far down to the Arkansas River at the south edge of town. He passed the depot and turned right, hoping he was headed in the same direction Charlotte had gone—and was now hopefully headed back.

As he strolled along the riverbank, among cottonwoods and pines, he felt his worries ease away. No wonder she'd chosen to walk down here. It was peaceful, even with the thrumming of the town nearby. Birds sang from the trees, and when the breeze came up, it ruffled the long grasses and made the heads of the wildflowers bob. And then there was the river itself. Down below, it churned and rushed, still full with the spring melt.

Mark found his mind wandering toward pleasant thoughts, all of them including Charlotte—laughing at a joke he told, spinning across a makeshift dance floor at a church social, baking him one of her terrible pies, resting her hand gently on his arm, and gazing up at him with pink lips and closed eyes—

"Help!"

The word, sharp but distant, yanked him immediately from the musings running through his mind. Mark looked forward and behind, but there was no sign of the person who had called for help.

"Help!" It came again, this time cut off at the end and distinctly coming from the river.

Mark clambered over tree roots to stand at the edge of the bank. There was nothing save for the rushing water and the leaves and sticks it carried along with it to the left. To the right—

There! A smudge of color, bright pink against the churning brown-blue of the water, rose and fell in the distance. Someone had fallen in, and Mark didn't hesitate to pull off his boots and hat.

"Help!"

Mark nearly froze with recognition. It was Charlotte.

He didn't stop to think any longer. He jumped right into the rushing water and swam with it toward her.

Chapter Ten

THE ICY WATER CHOKED off Charlotte's scream.

She fought again to lift her head above the rushing tide of the river. Clearing the water again, she drew in a great breath as her heart slammed against the inside of her chest. Her shoes felt like weights, dragging her down as she kicked to remain afloat.

If only she'd been able to tag along with her brothers to swim in the ocean, maybe then she'd know what to do. All she knew right now was that she *had* to keep propelling herself upward. If only there were a tree limb or sturdy bush along the bank she could grab onto. But even that was a fruitless wish she could barely comprehend past the fight to simply keep her head above the water.

Just as it seemed a tidal wave had pressed her face under again, something sturdy locked around her waist. Charlotte gasped, drawing in the water she so desperately had fought to keep out.

The thing around her waist—*arms?*—pulled her upward, and she emerged again, sputtering and coughing.

"It's all right, I've got you," a voice said.

"M-Mark?" The name came out in a fit of coughing as she barely noticed she'd called him by his given name.

He tightened his grip around her as he swam with the current toward the bank. They reached a large, spring green bush that half hung over the river, and he grabbed hold of it, stopping them against the pull of the current.

"Can you reach it?" he asked.

With every ounce of energy she had left, Charlotte gripped great handfuls of the bush, and with one of Mark's arms still securely wrapped around her waist, she pulled herself closer to the bank using the shrub's branches.

She gritted her teeth and pulled as hard as she could to lift herself onto the bank. But even if she slipped and fell again, he would be there behind her to catch her. That knowledge warmed her, and she reached a hand out to dig into the soft dirt of the riverbank. She pulled herself up the rest of the way. Until, finally, she was safely on land again.

Charlotte lay where she was, gasping hard for breath and somehow coughing at the same time. Mark—no, Mr. Becker—appeared beside her, water dripping from the ends of his hair, which looked longer than she'd realized it was, as he watched her with a set jaw and serious eyes.

She coughed again, and he took hold of her arms.

"You need to sit up. It'll be easier to catch your breath," he said, his hands warm and welcome over the sleeves on her arms.

She nodded, and he gently helped her sit.

Charlotte wished for a boulder or a tree trunk to lean against, but she remained sitting as she coughed again. He sat patiently beside her. When she finished yet another round of coughing, she found his hand resting on her forearm, a gentle weight that anchored her to solid earth.

"Better?" he asked when a moment passed without new coughing.

Charlotte nodded, afraid to speak or else her lungs might rebel again.

"I'd like to make a joke about why you decided to go for a swim, but I fear it would be too funny and would make you choke again," he said with a smile tugging at the corner of his lips.

His words made her smile too, and she bit her lip to keep that grin from turning into a giggle. The breeze picked up, lifting the tiny strands of hair that had already dried. She'd lost her hat to the river, but at least it wasn't the new one she'd only just purchased.

The breeze came again, stronger this time, and Charlotte shivered as the cooling air of evening cut straight through her wet clothing.

Mark moved closer and wrapped an arm around her shoulders. Charlotte gave up trying to think of him as *Mr. Becker* as she sank gratefully into his warmth. The scent of tobacco and soap was just barely there, and it made her relax immediately. There was something that felt so safe, being here in his arms. As if no one or nothing could ever harm her or force her to do anything she wished not to do.

"Thank you," she said finally. She tilted her head back to see his face. "For rescuing me."

"I'm thankful I came by when I did. The woman at the boarding house said you'd come down here." His voice, steady and low, warmed her from head to toe.

"I grew impatient and came for a walk." It felt foolish to say aloud, but how was she to know a simple walk would end with her slipping on the bank and falling into the river? "Did you speak with the sheriff?"

"He confirmed what we'd thought. The McNabs left town a while back. Apparently Mr. McNab wasn't entirely honest when it came to dealings with local businesses."

Charlotte bit her lip again, trying to make sense of it. None of this matched what she knew about Ruby.

But then again, how well did she really know Ruby?

"Well, I hope she's all right, wherever she is." It seemed that was all she could say. She was hardly about to pass judgment until she knew more, and she may never know more.

It seemed it was time to end her search for the woman she'd thought of as a friend, and decide what she might do with her life now that returning home seemed to not be an option.

"What sort of work do you suppose I'm suited for?" She turned her gaze back up to Mark. The money she'd taken from home wouldn't last forever. She would need to earn more eventually.

He blinked, as if her question had caught him by surprise. Then he smiled, and the simple encouraging warmth of it set her mind at ease again.

"I imagine you're suited for any work you might wish to do, Charlotte." Her name, spoken in his low, calming voice, made her skin grow goose pimples, even under the heat of his arm wrapped around her shoulders.

No one had ever said such a thing to her. Because no one had ever believed in her courage or intelligence the way Mark did. A rush of affection surged through Charlotte, and she suddenly yearned for him to kiss her.

But he didn't, of course, because he was far too much the gentleman.

And so, before she could think or remember that she was a sensible person, she lifted her head and stretched just far enough to kiss him instead.

He seemed to freeze as her lips found his. Charlotte nearly froze herself. What was she doing? She'd never kissed a man before, if one discounted the overly eager Mr. Goyette last year, who mistook her kindness for affection.

But it took only a second before Mark's other hand found the back of her neck and he pulled her closer. Charlotte felt as if she were somehow falling and floating at the same time. His kiss was tender with some barely suppressed urgency, and she rested her hands against his chest as she fought to keep herself grounded.

He made a sound somewhere deep in his throat and pulled away, gazing down at her as if she were something entirely surprising.

And that's when she realized exactly what she'd done. Her face went warm, and she scrambled to her feet.

"Charlotte?" he said.

But she was already running as fast as her heavy, wet skirts would let her, back to the safety of the boarding house.

Chapter Eleven

THE SUN HUNG LOW IN the sky as Mark watched Charlotte disappear toward town. The touch of her lips against his lingered, and his arms felt empty without her in them. She hadn't even looked backward as she'd run away.

What had he done?

Nothing. Well, nothing except fall headlong into what she'd given him. She couldn't be angry with him for that, could she? She certainly didn't seem upset in the moment. Nor did she look at him as if she was mad at him afterward.

It had to be something else.

And he had to find out what it was, or at least ensure she was all right. He made his way along the river, back toward the depot, walking at a slower clip to make sure he gave Charlotte enough time to return to the boarding house and sort through her thoughts.

It was nearly sunset when he arrived. The door to the boarding house was already locked for the night. The woman who usually sat at the desk answered his knock.

"It's too late for visiting," she said with her usual friendly smile. "You'll have to come back in the morning."

Mark couldn't imagine sitting with this uncertainty all night. If Charlotte felt the same about him as he felt about her, he needed to know *now*. Or, at the very least, he had to make sure she didn't despise him. If he didn't, he wouldn't get a wink of sleep.

"I'll only be a moment, I promise. Please."

She eyed him a moment, and then opened the door just wide enough for him to slip through. "I'll fetch Miss Montgomery. Five minutes, and then you must leave."

He nodded gratefully and waited in the doorway of the parlor. He was far too antsy to take a seat.

Not more than a minute later, the woman's footsteps sounded on the stairs.

"Miss Montgomery did not answer the door. I presume she's gone to sleep," the woman said when she reached the bottom step.

It was hardly late enough to turn in for the night. Mark glanced past the woman to the stairs, as if he could suss out why Charlotte didn't answer simply by looking up to the second floor.

"I'll be just a moment." And moving quickly so that he couldn't change his mind and the proprietor couldn't stop him, he bounded around her and up the stairs.

"Sir!" Her normally friendly voice had grown much sharper. "Sir, you can't go up there!"

He cringed at the thought that he might be the reason that poor woman wound up hiring someone to keep out men just like him, who broke the rules with hardly a second thought.

But he *had* to know. He couldn't wait until morning.

Once on the landing, he looked right and left. Which room was Charlotte's?

"Sir, *please*." The boarding house proprietor's eyes were wide with anxiety. "You can't be up here. You'll make my guests fearful."

"This won't take long, I promise. I just have to speak with her. Which room is Miss Montgomery's?"

"As if I'm going to tell you *that*." She crossed her arms, and gave him a look that said she'd sooner toss him down the stairs than relay that bit of information.

"I could knock on each door—"

Before he could finish, the door immediately to his left opened, just far enough for Charlotte to see him.

"Whatever is going on out here?" she asked.

"I tried to keep him downstairs," the proprietor said. "But he pushed right past me and refused to leave."

Charlotte stared at him as if she didn't recognize him at all, and Mark's face felt as if it had caught fire. She must think him as uncouth as the boarding house owner clearly thought he was.

"My apologies," he said, stumbling over the words. "I simply wanted to ensure Miss Montgomery was all right." He paused. "Are you? All right, I mean?"

Her expression softened. "Yes. I'm sorry I worried you."

It was difficult to be frank with the owner of the boarding house standing right there. "I . . . I enjoyed our walk. I hope you did also," he said somewhat stiffly, hoping it conveyed what he truly meant.

She pressed drying hair away from her face as her skin tinged pink. "Yes, I did. I suppose I worried that you didn't. Or that you might think me someone I'm not."

So that was why she'd run. She was embarrassed and feared he'd think her too forward. Mark couldn't suppress his smile. He swept his hat in front of him as if he were bowing to her. "Miss Montgomery, I'd be pleased to take a walk with you any time you'd like."

Charlotte smiled at him then—a genuine grin of the sort that had made him take leave of his senses when he first met her. "I'm glad to hear that."

"Mr. Becker, sir. Please, you must go now." The boarding house proprietor's look of confusion about the entire situation finally gave way to an irritated urgency, as if every woman in the place was about to look out her door and raise a fuss about them conversing in the hallway.

"Yes, I will," he said to her. "Thank you for your hospitality. Miss Montgomery, I'll call on you again tomorrow."

The proprietor followed him down the stairs, not at all trusting him to leave on his own, he supposed. But when he glanced back up the stairs, Charlotte still watched him from the door.

As he stepped out into the darkening evening, Mark was fairly certain he'd dream about that kiss for all his days to come. He whistled as he crossed the road to his own boarding house. If Charlotte didn't want to return home, perhaps she would remain here. He could stay in town too, find some other work nearby. They could get to know each other even better.

Nothing could dampen his spirit now that he knew Charlotte enjoyed his company as much as he enjoyed hers. Not even thoughts of how Mr. Montgomery might react if he discovered what had happened.

Chapter Twelve

WITH ONE DRESS DRYING from the wash after its dip in the Arkansas River and another not yet made, Charlotte had the choice of exactly one skirt and one shirtwaist the following evening—the ensemble she already wore. She looked down at the serviceable navy blue skirt and lacy white shirtwaist. They were fashionable enough, she supposed, not that it mattered so much out here. It was sort of freeing, in fact, not to have to worry about keeping up with the latest in hems and sleeves. Besides, she looked perfectly fine in this clothing, even if her mother would have shuddered at the thought of her wearing a day dress to dinner.

Worries about what she wore wouldn't have even crossed her mind if Mark hadn't sent around a note saying he would take her out for dinner this evening. The little missive with his careful printing had made her smile so much that one of the other girls staying at the boarding house had asked if she had a suitor.

She'd foolishly smiled again and again for no reason throughout the day until it was time to excuse herself to her room to prepare. Not that she had much to prepare, but a quick splash of water on her face and a freshening up of her hair made it feel as if she were doing something right.

At precisely six o'clock, she went downstairs to await Mark's arrival in half an hour. It was early, but she supposed it would be better to while away the time chatting with some of the other girls instead of pacing about her room in nervous anticipation.

What would Mama and Papa think about all of this? Her sister Mary would be overjoyed, and Charlotte was certain Mary would adore Mark. But her parents . . . Charlotte frowned as she imagined their reactions. Mama would utterly disapprove of a man with "such little means," and Papa would outright forbid it—particularly since he was paying Mark to look after her.

But they weren't here, she thought as she swept into the parlor. Which meant she could do as she pleased, including having dinner with one particularly kind and handsome gentleman.

She took a seat next to one of the other girls, who was engaged in a lively conversation with two other young women who stayed at the boarding house. Charlotte tried to pay attention to the topic, which had something to do with an upcoming church social, but she found her mind wandering again.

Thoughts of Mama and Papa had made her wonder exactly what Mark was telling her father—or what he *would* tell her father. If they kept on having dinner and going on walks and . . . well, taking *walks*, he'd have to say something to Papa eventually. And Charlotte shuddered to think of how well that would go over.

She shouldn't let it bother her. After all, if she wasn't returning home, she needed to forge a life for herself somehow.

And why shouldn't it be here? Why shouldn't it be with Mark
. . . if he were to ask, anyhow.

She looked down at her hands, her face going warm at the
very thought. But she determined to put her parents from her
mind. If it came time to tell Papa, then so be it. And hopefully
they would come around to the idea once they had time to get
used to it.

"Charlotte?" One of the other girls stood at the door, a
folded sheet of paper in her outstretched hand.

Charlotte jerked her mind from her thoughts and stood.
"Is that for me?"

The other woman nodded. "It came just a moment ago. A
young boy delivered it without a word."

That was curious. Perhaps it was Mark, advising her of
some delay in their plans for dinner. Charlotte took the note
and thanked the girl. Standing just inside the doorway to the
parlor, she unfolded the paper.

It was not at all what she'd expected.

With a hand going involuntarily to her mouth, Charlotte
read the note again.

Dearest Friend,

*Please, I need your help. Find me around the rear of the
Methodist Church on Macon Ave. Do hurry. I cannot wait for
long, and the situation is dire.*

The note was unsigned, but Charlotte knew it was from
Ruby. Who else in Cañon City would send her such a note?

She pinched the paper between her fingers as her heart
raced. Ruby was in trouble. She needed help. And she needed
it quickly. Charlotte *knew* Ruby couldn't have been the one
behind stealing that money at the restaurant. That wasn't the

woman she'd known back in Baltimore. It must have been a misunderstanding. And now . . .

Show it to Mark first. That was the most practical course of action. Mark could help. He could, at the very least, go with her to the church. Because if there was even the slightest chance this was Ruby, Charlotte was not leaving her alone to face whatever trouble she'd found.

If it wasn't Ruby . . .

She didn't much want to think on that even as she had to acknowledge it was a possibility. Swallowing the fear that rose in her throat, Charlotte slipped out of the parlor just as the front door opened to reveal Mark.

"Oh, thank goodness!" Relief rushed out of her as she stepped toward him. He cut a handsome figure in a nice black suit, and Charlotte couldn't help but let her eyes trace the width of his shoulders even as she handed him the note.

"What's this?" He read it quickly, then read it a second time.

"It's Ruby. We must go," Charlotte said, stepping around him to the door.

He reached out and laid a hand on her arm, shaking his head.

"No."

Chapter Thirteen

MARK WITHDREW THE HAND he'd placed on her arm with some effort. He didn't know how his mind went immediately to pulling her close for a kiss, but creating a little space between them helped him wrench his thoughts back to the question at hand.

"How do you know this is from Mrs. McNab? It's unsigned," he asked.

"I can't be certain, of course, but it must be from her. Who else would send me such a message?" Charlotte twisted her hands together. "I'm worried about her. What if something terrible happens before we can get there?"

Mark glanced down at the note again. It didn't appear hurriedly written, which felt odd for a note that conveyed such urgency in its words. Yet every letter was carefully created, without a single stray splotch of ink, smudge, or mistake.

Something about it felt . . . off.

When he looked back up at Charlotte, she was biting her lip as worry darted across those big brown eyes.

"Let me look into it first. I'll get the sheriff and go to the church. But I need you to remain here." He folded the note and handed it back to her.

"You keep it," she said. "The sheriff may wish to see it."

Relief at her words washed through him. He'd thought for certain Charlotte would insist upon coming, and the last place he wanted her was headed into what could be danger. But for all of her brazen acts upon arriving in Cañon City, she did have a good head on her shoulders, and for that, he was thankful.

"You'll stay here?" he asked, just to make certain.

She nodded, then gave him a little smile. "I suppose we'll have our dinner another evening."

"Of course." He paused, holding her dark eyes with his own as affection surged through every bone and muscle in his body. "I look forward to it." All of his hopes for finding out more about her feelings toward him, his yearning to discover even more about her, and his desire to simply spend time looking into those eyes and imagining all the possibilities the future had would simply have to wait.

She pressed her lips together as if she were nervous before taking his hands. "Please be careful, Mark. I believe this is Ruby, and I believe she truly is in trouble, but if it isn't her . . ." Her fingers tightened around his.

Glancing around to find no one nearby and the ladies in the parlor hidden from their view, Mark leaned down and placed a kiss on her forehead.

"Don't fret about me. I'll be just fine." He let a hand linger on her cheek. She closed her eyes, and it took all of his self-control to pull his hand away.

"Have some dinner here," he said as he opened the door. "I'll return soon."

She watched him as he stepped down to the street, and when he turned again, the door was closed with Charlotte safely inside.

Sliding the note into his pocket, Mark turned toward the sheriff's office.

It was time to find out what was going on with Mrs. Mc-Nab and her husband, once and for all.

Chapter Fourteen

HOURS PASSED, TIME dragging as slowly as it did when Charlotte was a child and waited for their cook to finish baking a batch of cookies.

She ate dinner with the other ladies, barely tasting any of the food, and then retreated to her room instead of the parlor. But that turned out to be a mistake, as she found her thoughts focused solely on Mark and Ruby, with no distraction at all to keep her mind from stumbling upon every terrible possibility.

What if someone had threatened Ruby and followed her to the church?

What if Mr. McNab had turned into a terrible husband and took his rage out on Mark?

What if the men Mr. McNab hadn't paid had finally had enough and were using Ruby to exact some sort of revenge?

What if Ruby and her husband were innocent but had fallen in with some bad people?

What if those people came to the church and began to shoot?

She shook her head, trying to clear it as she opened the window. Great gulps of fresh air helped clear away the dime novel scenes playing through her mind, one after the other.

Charlotte rested her hands on the window sill and examined the dark outlines of buildings and gray shadows of clouds in the moonless night. Mark was smart and capable, and he would have the sheriff with him. All would be well. And perhaps they'd even be able to help Ruby.

She would find all of her worry was for naught.

A breeze lifted the ends of the hair she'd so carefully prepared for her outing with Mark. Perhaps she should return downstairs. Surely some of the girls were still whiling away the evening in the parlor. Sometimes they retreated back to the dining room for card games. That would be a good distraction, much better than trying to still her runaway mind by looking out the window at the oppressive black of the night.

Mind made up, Charlotte closed the window and moved to her door. As she crossed the landing and made her way down the stairs, she forced her thoughts back to the dinner that didn't happen. She'd so looked forward to trying to discern more of Mark's feelings toward her. Were they fleeting, or were they of the serious sort?

She *so* hoped it was the latter. He didn't seem the sort of man to toy with a lady's feelings, anyhow. And he'd come running all the way over here last night, risking his reputation and his welcome at this boarding house by insisting on coming up to her room to find out if she was all right.

A man who didn't care deeply for a woman wouldn't do such a thing, would he?

Charlotte decided that indeed, he would not, and although she still exercised caution over losing her heart to him, she thought it wouldn't hurt to let a little hope brighten her thoughts for the future.

Provided he returned safely.

And *that* was precisely the kind of thinking she needed distraction from.

When she peered into the dining room, she was pleased to find a game of cards in full swing. Settling herself down next to one of the younger girls, she waited for them to finish the round.

A minute passed. Then two. Then five. Ten minutes, and Charlotte found herself twisting her hands together in her lap, all of those terrible scenarios running again through her mind.

"I'll be right back," she said as she rose. "I just need to get some air."

The girl dealing the cards nodded. "You can rejoin us in the next round."

Charlotte nodded gratefully. She'd get air, clear her mind again, and then lose herself in the game.

Outside, the wind blew strongly enough to ruffle her skirts and send wayward sticks of straw dancing across the board sidewalk. Charlotte drew in a breath, letting it fill her and slow her heart as she closed her eyes.

He would be just fine.

He'll return at any moment.

She felt much better when she opened her eyes again, and she could even smile as she pictured the owner of the boarding house discovering the door unlocked and Charlotte standing outside like a wild woman in the wind.

Heart beating normally again, Charlotte turned to go inside when a voice stopped her still.

"Charlotte?"

She turned, and there, at the foot of the steps down to the sidewalk, stood Ruby.

It was so unexpected that Charlotte didn't know whether to laugh or cry out in concern. But her friend from Baltimore smiled at her, and before Charlotte knew it, she'd rushed forward to embrace her.

Ruby looked a fright, her pretty blonde hair a mess of tangles and her skirts torn and stained, even in the dim lamplight shining through the windows from the boarding house.

"Are you all right?" Charlotte asked. "I received a note, and I thought it might be you."

Ruby's eyes darted to the left and the right, as if she expected to see someone standing there and listening to their conversation. Finally, they landed on Charlotte again as she clasped her hands in front of her.

"That was me," she said with a nervous lick of her lips. "But I didn't see you there so I thought I might come here instead."

Why didn't she ask Mark or the sheriff for help? They ought to have been at the church by now. But as Charlotte appraised her friend's skittish appearance again, she wondered if Ruby hadn't been too afraid to talk to anyone except Charlotte. After all, she didn't know Mark or the sheriff.

But she knew Charlotte.

Charlotte reached for her friend's hand. She wore no gloves, and her fingers were chilled, even on such a warm night. "Tell me, Ruby, what's happened? How can I help you?"

Ruby looked down, as if she were thinking, before raising those nervous eyes up to Charlotte again. "Please, I need you to come with me."

"To where? Should we get the sheriff first?"

"No, no, please." Ruby shook her head so quickly that her hair bobbed with the motion. She wore no hat either, which was particularly odd. Ruby had always been one so careful with her appearance, much more so than Charlotte herself. "We mustn't involve the law. *Please.*"

Charlotte's heart sat uneasy in her chest. What was so terrible that Ruby would refuse the help of the sheriff?

"Does this have something to do with the restaurant? I'm certain Sheriff Young would—"

"No . . . Yes. Perhaps a bit. You'll understand when you see. Please come with me?" The pleading in Ruby's voice had reached a level of desperation.

Charlotte's teeth worried her bottom lip as she looked back at the boarding house door. Mark had asked her to remain here. If he returned, and she'd gone, what would he think? Yet she could hardly walk inside and inform the other girls she was headed out to help a friend who might very well be wanted by the law. And if she simply told them she was going for a stroll, they'd likely think she'd lost her mind and insist she remain put.

Looking back at Ruby's face—were those tear stains tracing lines down her dirty cheeks?—Charlotte made up her mind.

Ruby was clearly desperate for her help, and Charlotte was not the sort to leave friends without aid when they most needed it. She would go with Ruby, find out what was the matter, and then return quickly to the boarding house—hopefully before Mark arrived.

With one last glance down the road to ensure he wasn't on his way now, Charlotte nodded. "Let's move quickly," she said.

"Oh, *thank you.*" Ruby clasped her hand as if it were a rock in a stormy sea. "I promise it won't take too long, but you must see it in order to understand."

Charlotte tried to make sense of Ruby's words as they walked and her friend seemed to withdraw into herself again. And she suppressed the feelings of doubt that rose the closer they got to the edge of town.

Despite her friend's mysteriously shoddy appearance and the rumors that she and Mark had discovered, Charlotte had no reason to doubt this woman she'd known for years.

Or so she hoped.

Chapter Fifteen

THE WIND NEARLY WHIPPED Mark's hat from his head as he approached the boarding house. Going to the church had been fruitless. No one was there, and by the time Sheriff Young suggested the note had been a hoax, they'd wasted nearly three hours.

All Mark wanted now was to see Charlotte, find a hot beverage and something to eat, and fall into bed—in that order.

Lamplight still shone from the windows in the boarding house. It was most certainly too late for visitors—again—but Mark knocked anyway. One of the young women Mark recognized as a guest answered the door. At least it wasn't the proprietor this time. He wasn't certain she'd let him get by her twice.

The girl at the door tilted her head as Mark said hello. "I believe Charlotte has gone upstairs for the night," she said.

"Would you mind asking her to come down? I know she'll want to see me."

The lady paused, then nodded and opened the door to allow him inside. "Don't tell Mrs. Barr," she said with a little giggle.

He stood outside the parlor after peering inside and being met with the gazes of at least seven unmarried young women, all of them at least somewhat curious about his presence.

The woman he'd spoken with returned a few minutes later. "I'm sorry, she isn't answering. She must be asleep."

Mark pulled out his pocket watch. "It's not even nine o'clock."

The woman shrugged. "I couldn't rouse her through the door."

"Is it locked?" he asked.

"Her door?" When he nodded, she added, "I'm not certain."

"I apologize for being so persistent, but it's urgent. Would you mind trying?"

She gave him a look that dripped with curiosity. "I suppose."

Mark waited another few minutes, tamping down the urge to run upstairs and check himself. The ladies in the parlor whispered, and he didn't dare turn around to meet their stares again.

Finally, after what seemed like an eternity, the woman returned downstairs. But this time, she frowned.

Mark stepped forward, the women in the parlor forgotten. "What happened?"

"It was unlocked, so I opened the door and . . . Well, she isn't in there."

"She said she was going outside earlier, when we were all playing cards," one of the women in the parlor said. "But I never saw her come back inside."

The woman next to her nodded. "I assumed she'd gone upstairs to sleep. She seemed very distracted all throughout dinner. I thought perhaps she was tired."

"Has anyone seen her since then?" Mark asked, his fingers digging into the brim of the hat in his hands.

The women all shook their heads or said that they hadn't.

"Thank you for your help." He replaced his hat and made for the door, his mind going in six different directions, trying to determine where Charlotte might have gone.

"Please, are you going to find her?" the woman near the desk asked. "Otherwise, we'll all worry ourselves sick over her."

"I will," he promised.

He was the one who was supposed to keep her safe. He was being *paid* to ensure her protection. And here she'd disappeared. He'd let his guard down, and look what had happened.

As he stepped outside, worry began to snake its way through his mind, pushing away his anger at himself. He'd find her if it was the last thing he did in this life. All he had to do was think through the possibilities.

It was late evening when Charlotte had left. Where could she have gone? And *why*? He knew she would be waiting for him, to find out what he'd discovered. Why would she disappear before then?

What if she was coerced? Or snatched off the street like an abandoned sack of goods? His heart clenched at the thought of her in any danger. If anyone hurt Charlotte, so help him, he'd ensure they paid.

Slow down, he told himself as he strode down the street. Charlotte had ventured into the most dangerous of places when she first arrived in town. She likely wouldn't think anything at all about venturing out in the dark for . . . what, exactly? What would entice her to leave the comfort of the boarding house when she knew he would return for her?

The shops were closed. She wouldn't have needed dinner. She had no use for a horse—Mark didn't even know if she could ride. It was too late to go visiting. She didn't know enough people to be invited to a party.

He worried his fingers against the edge of his pocket. There wasn't a place he could think of where she might have gone . . . but perhaps it hadn't been to a *place*.

Maybe it had been with a person.

Mark picked up speed, glancing down alleys as he passed, making his way from one street to the next until he'd covered most of the town.

Fear gnawed at the edges of his senses.

That note had felt *wrong* to him. Couple that with the fact that no one had been there the entire time he and Sheriff Young had waited, and the entire situation was suspicious. They'd spent so much time waiting that Charlotte had disappeared right out from under him.

Unless . . .

That was the point. If he was distracted, and the person who sent the missive *knew* he wouldn't allow Charlotte to accompany him, that was the perfect opportunity for them to lure Charlotte out of the boarding house to . . . somewhere.

He didn't know where she might have gone with this person—or people—but he would find them.

Mark turned on his heel and strode toward the sheriff's office.

He would find her, and he would do it with the full force of the law behind him.

Chapter Sixteen

THE EMPTY HOUSE AT the edge of town was empty for good reason.

In the time she'd been sitting on the floor in the corner of what Charlotte presumed was the unfurnished parlor, she'd heard the telltale signs of rodents scratching wood and had sneezed at least three times from dust. Not to mention the hole in the ceiling, through which she could see stars. The wind found its way through cracks in the walls, whistling and giving the house a good shake now and then. A single lamp, turned down low, made just enough light to keep the darkness outside from overtaking the house.

Ruby sat against the opposite wall, crying silently ever since they'd arrived. Charlotte couldn't decide whether she felt bad for the woman she thought had been her friend, or whether she was simply angry at Ruby's ploy to get her here.

And Charlotte had believed her—right up until they'd walked into the empty house and she'd found two armed men waiting. They'd grabbed hold of her, pushed her into the corner, and refused to let her leave. One was Bertram McNab. Charlotte barely recognized him with the scraggly beard and clothes that hung on a too thin frame. Then again, she'd only seen him once back in Baltimore, so she might not have recognized him even if he had looked himself.

The other man she knew only as Polson, which was how Mr. McNab referred to him. He was even meaner looking than McNab. The house apparently belonged to this Polson, who'd made quick work of asking McNab when they'd get paid for all this work.

What, precisely, they'd be paid for, and what Charlotte had to do with it all baffled her. After she'd swallowed her initial shock and anger at Ruby's betrayal, she'd tried to ask Ruby why she was here. But her husband had immediately told her to shush, and Ruby had skulked away to cower in the corner across the room.

"The sooner we get this into motion, the better." Polson leaned against the front door, presumably to keep Charlotte from leaving through it. At least he'd holstered his revolver, although his eyes kept flitting toward her, as if he didn't trust the way she was sitting quietly. She'd turned to run only one time, but Polson had grabbed her arm and dragged her back into the house. Despite the currents of fear that seemed to have overtaken her entire body, something in the back of her mind told her to be still.

If they thought they could trust her, she might find a way out of this.

"Ruby!" McNab snapped.

Ruby jerked, her eyes wide.

"You write this." He fished a stub of a pencil and an old crumpled sheet of paper from his pocket and dropped them onto the floor in front of her.

Slowly, Ruby reached down for the pencil. She flattened the paper against the floor and waited.

Charlotte shifted as McNab appeared to be thinking. She pressed her hand against the gritty floor and then immediately lifted it, not wanting to know what exactly she sat on. The floor was uncomfortable, to say the least. Polson's eyes flicked to her again, and she stilled, not wanting to draw his attention.

"To Mr. C. Montgomery," McNab said.

Charlotte froze, her breath catching in her throat as Ruby wrote down her husband's words. They were writing a letter to her father. And she feared she knew why, although her heart didn't want to believe it of Ruby.

"Asset is safe." He paused, looking up at the hole in the ceiling as he appeared to think. "For return, payment of . . . twenty thousand dollars—"

"Twenty-five," Polson interrupted.

McNab nodded. "Change that to twenty-five thousand dollars," he instructed Ruby. "By July first, or asset will be disposed of."

His gaze sliced over to Charlotte. She forced herself to remain rigid, her arms clasped around her bent knees and her face—she hoped—devoid of any expression. But inside, a panicked scream yearned to force its way out and her heart beat so hard she worried the men would hear it. She moved only to bite her lip to force the scream back down.

McNab smirked at her. "You're gonna make us rich men, Miss Montgomery."

Charlotte held his gaze until he looked away, back to Ruby. *Ruby.*

She must have heard that Charlotte was searching for her and shared that information with her husband. And he had then concocted this scheme with Polson. Ruby appeared remorseful for her part in all of this, but had she been all along? Or only when she realized what might happen to Charlotte if her father didn't follow through with payment?

Charlotte swallowed hard at that thought. He would do as the letter requested, wouldn't he? And then she'd be indebted to him for the rest of her life. That thought left a bitter taste in her mouth. She'd remain alive, but she'd be obligated to live that life back in Baltimore, married to Mr. Lindstrom. Her heart ached at the thought of leaving Mark behind.

"Good," McNab said, breaking into her thoughts. He handed the slip of paper back to Ruby, who was now standing. "Take that straight to the telegraph office. Then wait till you get a response, even if it takes all night."

Charlotte's stomach turned at the thought of sitting here alone with the two men for the duration of the night.

Ruby started for the door, but McNab grabbed her arm, hard enough that she almost tripped. Charlotte gritted her teeth at the action, wishing she could stand and give Mr. McNab a good slap across the face.

"Don't dawdle. And for the sake of Miss Montgomery, don't talk to anyone." He let her go and then nodded toward Polson. "Give her some money."

Polson scowled, but he reached into his pocket and withdrew some bills. Ruby walked almost silently across the floor, shooting a quick, desperate glance at Charlotte before taking the money Polson held out.

Ruby left, and Charlotte tried to be thankful they were sending by telegraph and not by post. And she prayed for a quick response, trying to shove aside the growing understanding that it would mean giving up her newfound freedom—and Mark.

As Polson and McNab conversed in whispers near the door, Charlotte fought to keep tears from her eyes. What if her father refused to pay? He likely thought of her as an ungrateful daughter, after all. If their scheme didn't work, she may not live much longer. That was terrifying enough, but if it did work, she would need to leave Mark behind.

And somehow, that felt even worse. Because if she left Mark here, she would be leaving her heart too. The woman who returned to Baltimore would be but a shell, an empty, obedient daughter.

Charlotte lowered her chin to her knees. She didn't pray this time.

Because she didn't know what to pray for.

Chapter Seventeen

LIGHTS WERE ABLAZE in the sheriff's office when Mark arrived. He shoved the door shut against the wind, and when he turned to greet Sheriff Young, he stopped still.

The sheriff wasn't alone. One of his regular deputies, Harry Caldwell, an older man who looked as if he'd tangled with more than his fair share of outlaws, was there, arms crossed and feet planted in a stance that would withstand the wind outside. But it wasn't Caldwell's presence that caught Mark off-guard.

It was the woman.

Petite, blonde, and without a hat, she looked as if she'd crawled out of a canyon on her hands and knees.

"Mark Becker," Sheriff Young said from where he leaned against his desk. "Meet Mrs. McNab. Mrs. McNab, Mr. Becker is the man assigned to protect Miss Montgomery."

Mark winced inwardly at the description of his job. Fine work he'd done at that. He'd grown too trusting, too sure of himself. Now Charlotte's life could be in danger. And if he had to hazard a guess, it would be at the hands of Mrs. McNab's husband.

"The church was a distraction," he said. It was a more a statement than a question, but the woman slowly nodded her head.

Tears filled her eyes and she looked down at the floor. "I'm sorry for that. I'm sorry for everything."

"Mrs. McNab brought us something very interesting." The sheriff handed Mark a slip of dirty, crumpled paper.

Mark skimmed the halting message. It read like a telegram, words condensed to lower the cost. He read it through again, and his blood thrummed in his ears.

"It's a note for ransom," he said in an even voice that barely disguised the anger and fear hidden below the surface. "For Char—Miss Montgomery."

"I didn't know what else to do." Mrs. McNab clenched her hands together, looking beyond pitiful in her torn skirts and tearstained face. "I couldn't send it. I've already done so much I wish I hadn't. I couldn't make it worse than it already was. So I came here."

"You made the right decision," Caldwell said, shifting his stance and looking distinctly uncomfortable at Mrs. McNab's watering eyes.

"Where is she?" Mark's words were barely restrained. Wherever it was, he wanted to run there, meet this McNab with his fists, and carry Charlotte out in his arms.

Mrs. McNab swallowed as she looked up at him. The fear in her eyes made him immediately regret the harshness in his words.

"The edge of town, far out Greenwood Avenue to the east," she said in a choked voice. "The last house on the left."

"I know the place," Young said. "Dilapidated. Used to be a fellow named Polson lived there."

"He's there now," she said. "Along with my— my husband." Fresh tears shimmered in her eyes.

"Anyone else?" Caldwell asked.

She shook her head.

"Are they armed?"

She nodded, seemingly incapable of words.

"I'm going," Mark said before Young could get a word out.

The sheriff nodded. "Harry, will you round us up some more men? We might be in need of help."

"What are we going to do with her?" Caldwell asked, finally dropping his arms.

The sheriff eyed Mrs. McNab. Mark wasn't sure if he'd ever seen anyone more pathetic in his life.

"She ought to go into one of those cells," Young finally said. "But I think she'd be better off upstairs with Penny."

"I deserve the jail," she finally said.

"You might, but go on up and get something to eat first." Young gestured at the nearby stairs, which led up to the rooms he lived in with his wife. "Penny will look after you."

The woman finally relented, and as soon as the door shut upstairs, they left, Caldwell turning right while Mark and the sheriff went to the left. They walked at a fast clip in silence, until they passed the last of the businesses.

"I don't know much about McNab," Young said. "I don't know if he's twitchy or calm. I don't know if he'll listen to reason or go down with the ship. Might be best to sneak up on the place rather than announce ourselves."

Mark nodded. "Whatever you say. I just want Miss Montgomery out of there as soon as possible, and unharmed." It was all he wanted. *She* was all he wanted. And if he got her out of there, he'd tell her that as soon as he could.

As the house came into view, they hung back. It was late enough that the few houses that were even remotely nearby were dark inside. What looked like a single lamp shone from somewhere in the front room of the house in question.

Young gestured at Mark, and they moved silently around the side of the house from a distance. The windows in the rear of the place were dark.

Mark glanced back toward the road. Where was Caldwell with the extra men? He shifted from foot to foot, ready to move, to do something, to get Charlotte out of there.

"Steady," Young said, his eyes never leaving the house. "They'll be here."

Mark clenched his fingers around the grip of the pistol at his side. Young was right. He knew that. It would be foolish to go it alone, and it might endanger Charlotte.

So he waited, a nervous, angry energy making it hard to remain still.

Finally, just as he was about to burst from the agony of waiting, Caldwell and three other men appeared like ghosts.

"I'm going to the back," Mark said, pulling his pistol.

Young nodded. "I'll cover the front. Caldwell, go behind Becker. The rest of you men spread out. We need people all around. But stay quiet. We don't want them knowing we're here until it's time."

Mark didn't wait another second.

He crossed the ground to the house silently, Caldwell on his heels, and climbed the half-rotten steps to the back door. Gripping the handle, he turned it ever so slowly.

And the door opened.

Chapter Eighteen

THE SECOND THE QUIET *click* came from the rear of the house, Polson leapt to his feet. He kicked the sleeping McNab in the leg until he woke.

"What's that?" McNab asked immediately.

Polson pressed a finger to his lips and gestured at the rear of the house and then at Charlotte.

Charlotte pulled herself into a ball as McNab stood and came toward her.

A small creaking sound came from what she presumed was the kitchen. Polson held his pistol out in front of him and made his way across the parlor. McNab gestured at her to stand. When she didn't comply, he reached down and dragged her up by the arm.

Heart pounding, she tried to pull herself from his grip, but he didn't relent. And when she saw the gun in his other hand, she stilled.

"Better drop your gun," Polson's voice sounded from the back room.

"On the contrary, you'd better drop yours."

Charlotte stifled a gasp. It was Mark! She hoped he hadn't come alone—he'd be outnumbered. If only McNab would let her go. Then she might be of some use.

"We just going stand here all night, aiming at each other?" Polson said.

"You planning to shoot first?" Mark replied.

With a grunt of impatience, McNab pulled her with him to the door that led to the kitchen. It was darker in that room, with the lamplight failing to penetrate the darkness. But Charlotte's eyes had already adjusted to low light, so it wasn't long before she could make out Mark, standing in front of the open back door, and Polson, immediately next to her.

Mark's gaze moved to her. "Charlotte. Are you all right?"

"Yes," she said in a voice she hoped wasn't tinged with fear.

"*Charlotte*, huh?" Amusement laced McNab's voice. "Finally found yourself a worthwhile suitor, Miss Montgomery?"

When she looked up at him, he fairly leered at her.

"Ruby told me how you didn't put much stock in those Baltimore dandies." He returned his gaze to Mark. "Not sure I'd put much stock in this one either, if I was you. Not too smart, seeing as how he's still standing there, even though we have him outgunned."

Charlotte couldn't make out Mark's expression, but he didn't move an inch. And it appeared he *had* come alone.

Which meant the only person he could rely upon for help was her.

And Charlotte would not let him down.

Without a second thought, she raised her foot and stomped down hard on McNab's toes. The sudden movement and surprise worked. He howled in pain and let go of her arm just enough that she was able to yank it away.

Before he could recover, she drew back her hand, intending to aim for his throat in the way her oldest brother had shown her years ago when she convinced him she wanted to learn how to fight.

But before she could follow through, a shot rang out.

A squeak flew from Charlotte's mouth as both she and Mr. McNab ducked. Next to her, Polson looked down in surprise at the hand that used to hold his revolver. It was now covered in blood, the gun on the floor.

Charlotte grabbed hold of his discarded pistol and pinned herself against the wall. Across the room, another man had appeared next to Mark, his revolver still smoking. Charlotte didn't recognize the man, but she did know what the star on his chest meant. He must be one of the sheriff's deputies.

Mark hadn't come alone.

Relief rippled through Charlotte. How many more men were there outside?

Out of the corner of her eye, McNab moved—toward her—breathing heavily with his gun outstretched.

"I want my money," he said.

Charlotte raised the pistol she'd picked up, her hands shaking. But before she could make the decision to pull the trigger, another shot rang out and McNab crumpled to the ground.

She stood perfectly still, watching him lie on the floor with a dark puddle forming around him. Two secure hands wrapped themselves around her arms, and half a moment later, one of them gently pulled the revolver from her hands.

"It's all right." Mark's voice, low and soothing, drew her attention away from the man on the floor. "He can't hurt you now."

"You shot him?" It was the only thing she could think to ask.

He nodded. "I didn't want to, but I wasn't about to let him hurt you."

Emotions surged through her, choking off the air. She fell into his arms as more men swarmed into the house and surrounded both McNab and Polson, who was still moaning in pain.

"You're safe now," Mark said in her ear.

She closed her eyes and breathed him in. He was everything to her, and she'd almost lost him. She could have ended up spending her life without him, but here he was. And here she was.

And nothing, she decided as she felt his arms tighten around her, would ever pull her away from him again.

"Mark," she said, tilting her head back. "I love you."

Chapter Nineteen

MARK HAD NEVER HEARD three such perfect words in his life.

With Charlotte's beautiful, trusting brown eyes looking up at him, he didn't care that anyone else was around them. He kept his arms around her and pressed his lips to her head.

"I love you too," he whispered against her hair.

She wrapped her hands around his arms and sighed. All he wanted to do was kiss her until everything around them disappeared. But he contented himself with holding her—for now.

"I was so worried about you," Mark said. *Worried* barely encapsulated the all-consuming fear he'd felt, knowing she'd been in danger. "When I found Mrs. McNab at the sheriff's office, I knew something was wrong."

"She went to the sheriff?" Charlotte smiled.

"She told us everything. I had the impression her husband wasn't the man she'd thought him to be."

"I'm glad. Now she'll be free of him."

"She'll likely face some charges of her own," Mark said. "As disinclined as it seemed Sheriff Young was to pursue them, he'll have to turn her over to the courts."

Charlotte worried her lip, making his thoughts go straight back to kissing her. "I'll speak on her behalf, if I'm allowed."

Mark's heart melted at her generosity. "Are you certain? She's the one who led you here and put you in this position."

"I'll talk to her first, but Mark, I think she regretted every second of it. And if she does, I'll speak for her. We all deserve forgiveness when we're truly sorry, don't we?"

He nodded before glancing behind her, where Caldwell and a couple of the other men were carrying McNab from the house.

"He's still alive," Caldwell said. "Don't know if he'll make it, but we'll take him to the doctor."

Mark swallowed, watching the nonresponsive man—the one who'd held Charlotte at gunpoint—lying still as he was carried from the house. He hoped he would be allowed forgiveness too, for shooting the man if he died. It was done to save Charlotte, but the thought that he had taken a life sat heavily on his soul.

"Mark?" Her soft voice brought him back.

"What about your father?" he asked, trying to leave the turmoil in his mind to deal with later, if McNab passed on.

She looked up at him. "He'll be angry, I imagine. But he'll either calm down and accept that I'm not coming home, or . . . he won't." She gave him a sad smile. "Perhaps Mary will be able to convince both him and Mama that I'm happier here."

"So you wish to stay here, in Cañon City?" Images of a life together began to flood his thoughts, pushing away thoughts of death and guilt.

She tilted her head to the side and studied him a moment. "Perhaps. Unless the man I love wishes to live elsewhere."

"Oh, you must mean Mr. Lindstrom." It felt good to tease her, especially when the smile stretched across her face.

"I didn't accept his proposal." She paused. "Although I suppose I could . . ."

Mark looked around at the dismal, dark house. This was a place of desperation and sadness. He wasn't about to ask her such an important question in here.

Instead, he took a step backward and dropped his arms to hold out one hand to her. "Come."

She took his hand and followed him out the door. Outside, Young and the two remaining men had found a horse for Polson.

The sheriff glanced between Mark and Charlotte. "Come see me tomorrow." And he gave them a knowing smile and began to lead the horse away, the other men, and McNab draped over another horse, following behind.

In the span of a few minutes, they were alone.

Charlotte looked up at him. "I believe you were going to tell me whether or not I should accept Mr. Lindstrom's proposal. Perhaps—"

She stopped speaking when he dropped to one knee.

"Charlotte," he started, suddenly feeling as if every word he planned to say sounded ridiculous in his head. He took a deep breath and began again. "Charlotte, I love you. And I want to spend the rest of my life with you. Making you laugh, saving you from whatever dark hovel you've ducked into for an adventure, and eating the terrible pie and tasteless cake you make and telling you how wonderful it is. Will you marry me?"

She covered her smile with her hand, and then nodded. "Yes. Yes, of course I will."

And with that, he rose, gathered her into his arms, and did what he wanted to do ever since he had first seen her. Ever since she'd kissed him. And ever since she'd arrived safely back in his arms. He dropped his lips to hers and savored every second. Her breath caught and a soft sigh escaped her lips. He pulled her even closer, and kissed her as if he would never have the opportunity to do so again.

When they broke apart, she leaned against his chest, as if she no longer had the strength to stand.

"I plan to do that at least fifty times a day for the rest of our lives," Mark said.

She looked up at him, her eyes soft and hazy in the darkness. "Well, then, I suppose we ought to get started."

He laughed, and then he kissed her again.

Epilogue

SIX YEARS LATER...

A crash sounded from the kitchen.

Charlotte dropped her broom and ran from the front hallway to the rear of the small house. The door to the pantry stood open, and a tiny head topped with dark curls peered out—and then disappeared again.

"Mama here," little Matthew's voice said in a loud whisper. At three, he followed his older sister around everywhere. And five-year-old Lillian had a penchant for trouble.

Steeling herself for a mess, Charlotte crossed the room. Inside the pantry, she found one little boy playing with flour as if it were the sand by the river—and one little girl covered head to toe in white.

Lillian looked sheepishly down at the flour jar, which was mostly empty but thankfully unbroken.

"Lillian?" Charlotte perched her hands on her hips and waited for an explanation on how dusting turned into the flour jar on the floor.

"It wasn't my fault," she said in her most angelic voice. "I was dusting it and it fell down."

Charlotte raised her eyebrows. It would take more than a swipe with a dust cloth to knock that jar off the shelf. "Are you certain? Because I'm not."

92

Lillian glanced down at her little brother. Sensing she was in trouble, she pulled Matthew back from the flour and held one of his little hands. "I may have dusted too hard. Or I moved it, maybe a little. I didn't mean for it to happen."

Charlotte nodded. "All right. Mistakes happen. You need to clean up the mistake though. After you help Matthew wash, you'll find the broom in the front hallway. And then the floor will need a good scrubbing. I'll bring the water in for that."

Looking like a pair of little ghosts, the children left through the back door, just as Mark entered.

"Dare I ask?" His eyes—of which Lillian's were a perfect copy—followed the children as they walked down to the well.

"Lillian dusted the flour right off the shelf." Charlotte swiped a hand across her forehead. "If I survive that child, it will be a miracle from God himself."

A sly grin crossed Mark's face as he reached for her hands. "You do know she's just like you?"

"Please don't remind me." Charlotte shook her head, this time in empathy for her mother and the string of nannies who'd helped raise her. She'd have to write Mama about this incident. It had taken some time for her parents to adjust to the idea of her remaining in Colorado—and marrying a man whose last name they'd never heard of. But from the moment Lillian was born and Charlotte had sent a photograph taken at Harper Photographic Studio back home to her parents, their letters hadn't ceased.

It was nice to have her family in her life again.

"She's good at finding trouble, just like a certain woman I know," Mark said.

"I don't find trouble anymore," Charlotte said with a mock indignant expression.

"Hmm." Mark looked her up and down. "Have you already forgotten about the church social?"

"*That* was because Sissy insisted she would organize the food, even though she'd already taken over the planning for the band and the dances. And you know how badly Mrs. Joliet wanted to be in charge of food, and I wasn't about to let Sissy simply take charge of *everything*!" Charlotte raised her chin. "That was not finding trouble. It was standing in defense of a friend's mother."

"And I had to hear about it for a week. I call that trouble."

"I'll show you trouble." And with that, Charlotte stood on her tiptoes and gave him one serious, long, and troublesome kiss.

"Oh, I like that kind of trouble," he said the second she broke away.

"Did Mama do something wrong?" Lillian's voice sounded from behind Mark.

Charlotte turned in his arms to face her daughter. Both Lillian and Matthew were dripping wet. "Of course not. I'm your mother."

Mark covered his laugh with his hand. Charlotte shook her head.

"Why don't you two wait outside and I'll bring you dry clothing?" she said, ignoring her husband.

The children obeyed, but before she could leave to retrieve a pair of towels and some clothing, Mark caught her hand and pulled her back to him.

"I love you and all the scrapes you get into," he said, pushing back a lock of wayward hair from her face.

"I should hope so. I plan to be stirring up all sorts of nonsense far into my old age," Charlotte replied.

"Good." He leaned down and kissed her again.

Charlotte could have easily lost herself in him, right there in the kitchen. "Our children are waiting," she said, her voice breathy when she pulled away.

He hung onto her fingers and she laughed.

"Fifty times a day, right?" she said.

"You owe me thirty kisses just for today," he called as she left the kitchen.

Charlotte ducked her head back around the doorframe. "You'll have to find me at the saloon."

His laughter followed her to the children's bedroom, and Charlotte laughed herself.

She'd cause him trouble until the day she died, so long as he kept coming to her rescue.

THANK YOU SO MUCH FOR reading! I hope you enjoyed Charlotte and Mark's story. Want to read even more of my sweet historical western books? A good place to start is with *Building Forever*[1], the first book in my Gilbert Girls series. (Sheriff Ben Young and his wife Penny meet in this series!)

To be alerted about my new books, sign up here: http://bit.ly/catsnewsletter I give subscribers a free download of *Forbidden Forever*, a prequel novella to my Gilbert Girls series. You'll also get sneak peeks at upcoming books, insights in-

---

1. http://bit.ly/BuildingForeverbook

to the writer life, discounts and deals, inspirations, and so much more. I'd love to have *you* join the fun!

Turn the page to see a complete list of my books.

More Books by Cat Cahill

Crest Stone Mail-Order Brides series
A Hopeful Bride[1]
A Rancher's Bride[2]
A Bartered Bride[3]
A Sheriff's Bride[4]
The Gilbert Girls series
Building Forever[5]
Running From Forever[6]
Wild Forever[7]
Hidden Forever[8]
Forever Christmas[9]
On the Edge of Forever[10]
The Gilbert Girls Book Collection – Books 1-3[11]

1. https://bit.ly/HopefulBride

2. http://bit.ly/RanchersBride

3. https://bit.ly/barteredbride

4. https://amzn.to/3z0PWPr

5. http://bit.ly/BuildingForeverbook

6. http://bit.ly/RunningForeverBook

7. http://bit.ly/WildForeverBook

8. http://bit.ly/HiddenForeverBook

9. http://bit.ly/ForeverChristmasBook

10. http://bit.ly/EdgeofForever

The Gilbert Girls Book Collection – Books 4-6[12]
Brides of Fremont County series
Grace[13]
Molly[14]
Ruthann[15]
Norah[16]
Charlotte[17]
Other Sweet Historical Western Romances by Cat
The Proxy Brides series
A Bride for Isaac [18]
A Bride for Andrew [19]
A Bride for Weston[20]
The Blizzard Brides series
A Groom for Celia [21]
A Groom for Faith[22]
A Groom for Josie[23]
Last Chance Brides series

---

11. http://bit.ly/GilbertGirlsBox

12. https://amzn.to/3gYPXcA

13. http://bit.ly/ConfusedColorado

14. https://bit.ly/DejectedDenver

15. https://bit.ly/brideruthann

16. https://amzn.to/3IyJRuA

17. https://amzn.to/3ArRtgD

18. http://bit.ly/BrideforIsaac

19. https://bit.ly/BrideforAndrew

20. https://bit.ly/BrideforWeston

21. http://bit.ly/GroomforCelia

22. http://bit.ly/GroomforFaith

23. https://bit.ly/GroomforJosie

A Chance for Lara[24]
A Chance for Belle[25]
The Matchmaker's Ball **series**
Waltzing with Willa[26]
Westward Home and Hearts Mail-Order Brides **series**
Rose's Rescue[27]
Hazel's Hope[28]
Matchmaker's Mix-Up **series**
William's Wistful Bride[29]
Ransom's Rowdy Bride[30]
The Sheriff's Mail-Order Bride **series**
A Bride for Hawk[31]
Keepers of the Light **series**
The Outlaw's Promise[32]
Mail-Order Brides' First Christmas **series**
A Christmas Carol for Catherine[33]
The Broad Street Boarding House **series**
Starla's Search[34]

---

24. https://amzn.to/3sAj0IV

25. https://amzn.to/3bYgQ1t

26. https://bit.ly/WaltzingwithWilla

27. https://bit.ly/RoseRescue

28. https://amzn.to/3o3P71P

29. https://bit.ly/WilliamsWistfulBride

30. https://amzn.to/3s0Lqwq

31. https://bit.ly/BrideforHawk

32. https://bit.ly/OutlawsPromise

33. https://bit.ly/ChristmasCarolCatherine

34. https://amzn.to/32sQuPS

About the Author, Cat Cahill

A SUNSET. SNOW ON THE mountains. A roaring river in the spring. A man and a woman who can't fight the love that pulls them together. The danger and uncertainty of life in the Old West. This is what inspires me to write. I hope you find an escape in my books!

I live with my family and a houseful of dogs and cats in Kentucky. When I'm not writing, I'm losing myself in a good book, planning my next travel adventure, doing a puzzle, attempting to garden, or wrangling my kids.

Made in United States
Troutdale, OR
08/05/2023

11837657R00065